RAIDERS OF THE MISSION SAN JUAN

On the trail of the Shannon gang, Marshal Lincoln Hawk learns that they have already been killed. Believing that the dead outlaws have been incorrectly identified he continues on the owlhoot trail. He finds the gang still very much alive at the Mission San Juan, preparing to claim a stash of Mexican gold. Whilst the gang fiercely protect their alibi, no help is forthcoming from the peaceful mission padres. As Lincoln confronts an army of gun-toting raiders can he hold his own?

SCOTT CONNOR

RAIDERS OF THE MISSION SAN JUAN

Complete and Unabridged

LINFORD
Leicester

First published in Great Britain in 2010 by
Robert Hale Limited
London

First Linford Edition
published 2011
by arrangement with
Robert Hale Limited
London

British Library CIP Data

Connor, Scott.
    Raiders of the Mission San Juan. - -
(Linford western library)
1. Outlaws- -Fiction. 2. Western stories.
3. Large type books.
I. Title II. Series
823.9′2–dc22

ISBN 978–1–4448–0732–5

Published by
F. A. Thorpe (Publishing)
Anstey, Leicestershire

Set by Words & Graphics Ltd.
Anstey, Leicestershire
Printed and bound in Great Britain by
T. J. International Ltd., Padstow, Cornwall

This book is printed on acid-free paper

1

The showdown was imminent.

To bolster his confidence Cameron White spread out his cards to look at his four queens, the best hand he'd ever had. Then over the tops of the cards he considered the other players.

Sitting opposite him was Billy Maxwell. The stern-faced man was tapping his fingers on the table with an insistent rhythm while glaring at him. The drunk to his left had passed out two hands ago and was lying with his head resting on his arms while snoring loudly. The nervous doctor to his right had backed out of this hand. He was eyeing the huge pot on the table with consternation, perhaps judging that the stakes had become so high the real showdown would come after the cards had been laid down.

Cameron reckoned he was right.

This late at night only two other men were in the saloon and they weren't watching the poker game. The bartender was lurking in the shadows and a tall man was nursing a coffee at the bar with grim determination.

'Time's up,' Billy muttered. 'Bet or quit.'

Billy licked his lips with surly confidence and that decided it for Cameron. He pushed the last of his money into the pot and sat back.

One at a time Billy revealed his cards, and his hand was a better one than Cameron had expected, showing a full house, aces over tens.

'That's mighty fine.' Cameron narrowed his eyes with a hint that he was annoyed. Then he turned over his cards to reveal his better hand.

Billy's only sign of disappointment was a twitching right eye.

'Where did you get that hand?' he grunted.

'You dealt it,' Cameron said levelly, taking Billy's comment as the first hint

2

that he would accuse him of cheating.

Billy smirked as he gestured at the pot. 'So take your winnings.'

Billy pushed back his chair. One hand moved to grip the edge of the table and the other drifted out of view beneath it.

Cameron considered the heaped bills, judging that there was over $500 there, but also judging that the moment he touched them, Billy would go for his gun.

Cameron met Billy's eye as he raised his hands above the pot to show he wouldn't make a move for his gun, making Billy smile. Then he lowered his hands. They were a few inches away when an ominous thud sounded.

Billy's gaze flicked to the side to see that the drunken player had stirred from his slumbers and was now looking at him. More surprisingly he had pulled a gun out from under his arm and had slapped it on the table. And the gun was cocked and aimed at Billy's chest.

'Reach,' the man said, his tone

authoritative and containing no slurring, 'or I'll tear a hole through you.'

'What the — ?' Billy murmured as he raised his hands.

The man sat up straight while keeping his gun on Billy. Then he winked at Cameron, who returned a grateful nod to his friend, Jack Miller. Only then did Cameron pounce on the money and pile up the bills.

'Obliged for the game,' he said, now reckoning with relief that he stood a good chance of keeping the money and his life.

'You two are working together,' Billy murmured, looking from one man to the other.

'A wise move when facing you.'

Billy conceded this point with a shrug. Then with his hands raised he got to his feet and backed away from the table for three strides.

'Taking my money was only half the battle. Have you two got the guts to keep it?'

Billy settled his stance, considering

them with arrogant confidence despite the gun aimed at his chest.

Jack stood and moved a few paces from the table to join him in standing in clear space.

'We have,' he said. 'So drop your gun and kick it to me. Then we're leaving. If you follow us, it'll be the last thing you do.'

'I won't follow you.' Billy waited until Jack and Cameron breathed sighs of relief before snorting a hollow laugh. 'We'll settle it here.'

Jack cast a nervous glance at Cameron, who returned an uncertain shrug confirming that Billy's gamble was a good one. Neither he nor Jack was a killer, but the same couldn't be said for Billy, who rolled his shoulders then jerked his hand towards his holster.

Jack firmed his gun hand, caught in a moment of indecision, but neither man got to fire when a strident voice barked out.

'Touch that gun and die!'

Billy stilled his movement and the others turned to see that the tall man at the bar was now watching the show-down. He was leaning back against the bar, his coffee in one hand, a Peacemaker in the other. The gun was aimed at Billy's back.

Slowly Billy turned.

'Are you with them too?' he muttered.

'Nope, I'm Marshal Lincoln Hawk,' the man said. He took a steady pace away from the bar. 'And you, Billy Maxwell, escaped prisoner and member of the Lawrence Shannon gang, are under arrest.'

★   ★   ★

'Get in there and quit whining,' Lincoln said as he shoved his prisoner through the door of the sheriff's office.

Sheriff Griffith was sitting at his desk. He looked up and smiled as he saw Billy come barrelling towards him.

Billy stuck out a leg to stop his

progress then swirled round to glare at the marshal, but this time he didn't waste his energy on another pointless attempt to attack his captor.

'You've got an ornery one there,' Griffith said, coming out from behind his desk. 'Where did you find him?'

'He was losing other people's money in a poker game at the saloon.'

Lincoln directed Billy towards the cells at the back of the sheriff's office. Griffith indicated the middle cell and, with only a brief protest when he stopped in the open doorway, Billy filed inside.

'What did he do?' Griffith asked as he locked the cell door.

'You should know more of the details than I do.'

'Why?' Griffith looked at the prisoner, his brow furrowing as he attempted to recognize him. His eyes narrowed as an idea came, but he shook the thought away. 'Nope. I've got no idea who he is.'

This comment made the prisoner sit on his cot with a self-satisfied gleam in his eyes and so, to avoid giving him any further hope, Lincoln drew the sheriff away from the cell.

'This is Billy Maxwell,' he said, his voice lowered. 'Last year he and his fellow gang members Keating Dobbs and Lawrence Shannon broke out of jail. Then six months ago on his own he roared through here. He killed two men and tried to burn Jim Hamilton's mercantile to the ground. I'd have thought you'd remember him.'

Griffith frowned. 'He does resemble the man I wanted for that crime. But he's not Billy Maxwell. That varmint got shot to hell two weeks ago.'

'He couldn't have,' Lincoln said, raising his voice so that even the prisoner could hear him. 'I've been tracking him and the rest of his worthless associates for a month.'

Sheriff Griffith shook his head. 'Then you've been following the wrong men. We cleared up the case to everyone's satisfaction. Jim Hamilton identified the body.'

Lincoln set his hands on his hips. 'Aside from Jim, who if I remember it right is blind in one eye and not seeing too good with the other, who also knew for sure the body was Billy's?'

Griffith folded his arms, showing that Lincoln's persistent questioning was irritating him.

'Judge Fleming. That good enough for you?'

Lincoln sighed. Fleming was no fool. He'd have been thorough before he declared the matter of identification closed, and he was also famed for not sanctioning bounty payments until every loose end had been tied up.

Lincoln leaned towards Griffith. 'Did you pay out a bounty on Billy?'

'Sure, to Richmond Cafferty and he doesn't make mistakes either.'

Lincoln frowned. His opinion of bounty hunters was only slightly higher than the outlaws they brought in, but if there was one man he didn't have utter contempt for, it'd be Richmond Cafferty.

He'd never met him, but for twenty years Richmond had brought in outlaws with a diligence any lawman would be proud of. Ultimately, he found everyone he set his sights on bringing to justice, even if it took him years.

'He's not made a mistake that I've heard about.' Lincoln waited until Griffith smiled. 'Until now.'

Griffith waved his arms in exasperation. 'Richmond's brought in over a hundred outlaws, but we still made sure he'd got the right man. And he had. Witnesses said so, I said so, the judge said so. Why do you know better than we do?'

Lincoln glanced at the prisoner, who was standing at the bars watching them with his head cocked to one side trying to catch their conversation.

'I don't,' he said, lowering his tone to a more conciliatory one. 'But I'm still asking you to keep him behind bars.'

Griffith tipped back his hat, sighing. 'I guess even if he's not Billy, he might have done something wrong. All right,

I'll keep him for two days and see if there's any chance we got it wrong.'

'Obliged.'

Griffith waggled a finger at him. 'But then, this man walks.'

2

'How much did we win?' Jack Miller asked.

'Seven hundred and sixty-three dollars,' Cameron White said.

'Let me see.' Jack strained his neck to look at the huge wad of bills. 'I've never seen that much money in my life.'

'Quit looking so eager.' Cameron looked up and down the deserted road to check nobody was showing an interest in them. 'We want to keep the money this time.'

They had come to Utopia, a day's ride from the scene of their unexpected windfall in Pandora, reckoning that it was sensible to put as much distance as they could between them and the events there.

They had been surprised that the lawman had let them keep the money they'd won. But he had decided that although Billy had probably stolen the money, they could take it as a reward for their help in catching him.

Even so, over the last few years the two friends had gained several windfalls at the poker table before going on to lose them, usually at the poker table again. So they took no chances that someone might try to take their money.

Only now that they were in a new town did they allow themselves to relax.

'What are we doing with it?' Jack asked, his eyes lighting up as his gaze turned to the many saloons along Utopia's main thoroughfare.

'Today we enjoy ourselves,' Cameron said. 'Then we set ourselves up in a nice little business. We're not frittering away this money.'

A stern frown replaced Jack's grin. 'Agreed. We were mighty lucky back there and I'm not risking getting shot to hell again.'

Cameron patted Jack's back. 'That's sensible talking, and a year from now, if

13

we invest wisely, we could double this money.'

That thought made Jack's grin return. 'In which case, I should keep it safe.'

Between the two of them, Jack was more proficient with a gun, so Cameron handed over the bills.

'Just keep it hidden and don't do anything foolish.'

'You can trust me,' Jack said, tucking the wad into an inside pocket. 'Nobody will ever know I've got nearly eight hundred dollars on me.'

Jack punched the air and then while grinning from ear to ear he beckoned for Cameron to choose which saloon they'd visit first.

Cameron considered his friend's beaming smile and eager eyes. Then with a sorry shake of the head that said he thought they'd be lucky to still have their money come sundown, he gestured at the nearest saloon.

★ ★ ★

Marshal Lincoln Hawk kicked open the door to the shack.

Four men were inside sitting at a table and sharing a jug of beer.

'Where's Keating Dobbs?' Lincoln demanded.

'Who wants to know?' the nearest man asked while eyeing him with surly contempt.

'Marshal Lincoln Hawk.'

The man sneered. 'A lawman who asks questions like that is either mighty stupid or a dead man. Which one are you?'

Lincoln offered a grim smile then paced inside.

These four men were the only people here. The only furniture was the table and the chairs they were sitting on. The only entrance was the door behind him.

'Then I must be mighty stupid,' Lincoln said. He waited until the man grunted a harsh snort. 'Because you haven't answered my question and I've let you live.'

The man glanced at his colleagues,

who all matched his arrogant posture by scraping back their chairs to give themselves room.

'If I tell you he's not here, will you scurry back into whatever hole you burrowed your way out of?'

Lincoln considered each man, but none of them matched the description he'd had of Keating Dobbs.

Sheriff Griffith's deadline still had a day to expire and the information that had led him here had been sound so he again noted the rude surroundings. When the bustling town of Utopia was only five miles away, four men wouldn't normally spend their evening here . . . unless they were waiting for someone.

'I know he's not here.' Lincoln smiled. 'I just want to know when he'll come.'

The man's expression became stern as Lincoln's question got to the truth.

'That's one too many questions,' he said. 'Here's the answer.'

The man's eyes narrowed, heralding

his next action, but a moment before he went for his gun Lincoln threw his hand to his holster. The other three men followed their lead but as they scrambled for their guns, Lincoln drew.

Four crisp shots rang out as Lincoln dispatched the guntoters.

The first two men received high shots to the chest that sent them tumbling from their chairs. The third man got a low shot to the guts that made him fold over to lie with his head on the table.

With time pressing the fourth slug slammed into the last man's shoulder, sending him wheeling into the wall.

Only the talkative man had the time to return a shot and that went winging over Lincoln's shoulder.

In three long paces Lincoln crossed the room then dragged the wounded man to his feet. He slammed the gun up under his chin and pressed in so firmly the man had to stand on tiptoes.

'Talk or die,' he said. 'When does Keating Dobbs get here?'

'I'm not saying nothing,' the man grunted through clenched teeth.

'Then you've got five seconds to live.'

Lincoln narrowed his eyes, his trigger finger twitching a mite to back up his promise. He started counting, but the man remained surprisingly calm.

When Lincoln reached four his gaze flicked over Lincoln's shoulder with a tell-tale sign that would have saved his life if he'd avoided making it.

Lincoln fired, blasting the man up and away from him, then turned and crouched. The man he'd shot in the guts was raising himself from the table and was swinging his gun up towards him.

With only a moment to react Lincoln caught the edge of the table with a flailing hand and upturned it, slamming the wood into the man's face and sending him reeling from his chair.

The man wasted a shot into the table before he hit the floor. Then he moved to get up, but Lincoln didn't give him a chance to fight back when he blasted a slug through the table and made the man screech before flopping.

Lincoln considered the man's still arms lying splayed out on either side of the table then the other three men. He judged that he wouldn't get any more surprises from them and so after he'd reloaded his Peacemaker he checked through the dead men's pockets.

None of the bodies had identification on them but he presumed that after he'd given their details to Sheriff Cushing in Utopia he would confirm they were all minor outlaws.

He headed to the door, resolving to lie in wait outside. He opened the door then flinched backwards for a pace when splinters kicked from the door-frame, the whine of a slug from outside echoing in his ears.

He just had enough time to see that more than one form was outside before he barged the door closed with his shoulder. He backed away.

'Who's in there?' a voice cried out from outside.

'Marshal Lincoln Hawk. Who's out there?'

A muttered conversation took place. Then barked orders sounded followed by shuffling feet as the men outside took up positions. Lincoln heard at least five separate people move around the shack.

'It's Keating Dobbs.' The voice came from a position side-on to the door. 'So for you it ends here.'

Another low order sounded, after which scurrying feet closed on the shack to stop beside the wall.

Lincoln presumed they were aiming to storm the building and take him, but with the door being the only way in, he reckoned that he could at least make Keating pay heavily for that assault.

With his gun trained on the door Lincoln waited quietly so as not to give Keating any clues as to his position when he burst in. But to his surprise when the man he'd heard earlier moved, he walked away from the building.

The first hint of what Keating had planned came when crackling sounded to his side. Then a whiff of burning wood came to him.

He looked to the base of the wall to see tendrils of smoke snaking up from the ground and through the cracks in the planks, the smoke becoming denser by the moment.

Lincoln backed away to the opposite wall, keeping the smoke in view as well as the door. He couldn't see flames and the wooden wall wasn't smouldering yet but the smoke was more than enough to cause problems. Great plumes rippled up to the roof where they coalesced to form a solid blanket.

There was no breeze coming through the door to disperse the descending cloud and so quicker than even Lincoln had expected he was coughing uncontrollably.

He dropped to his knees to buy himself a few more minutes and this did at least clear his throat, but to make this much smoke they must have piled a considerable amount of combustible material outside.

He couldn't sit out the attempt to smoke him out.

In the last moments before the gathering smoke took the walls from view he saw that the fire had now taken hold and the first lick of flame was reddening the wall.

Then he started to cough again. Even though Keating was waiting to kill him when he came out, he had to leave. But he reckoned the smoke that was causing him problems might also aid him by keeping him hidden for a few precious moments.

He crawled to the table and grabbed it. Then he took a deep breath and stood.

With the acrid smoke stinging his eyes he swung the table round to place it before him as a makeshift shield. It hadn't saved the man earlier, but it might deflect some of the slugs that were sure to come his way.

He turned to the door and set off,

but now the smoke was so thick he couldn't even see the door and he blundered into a wall. Heat licked at his hands and he realized he'd strayed close to the burning section. He flinched away, his motion swirling the smoke and letting him see that the flames had burnt through the wall.

He smiled to himself, deciding to do the unexpected, then launched the table at the burning wall. It crashed through, sending burnt wood in all directions and clearing a space that was big enough for Lincoln to dive through.

He followed the table and landed in the heap of burning branches and leaves, all thankfully smouldering more with smoke than flames, then kept rolling to escape the fire.

He came to rest five feet from the fire, his clothes fire-licked and burning, but he put that problem from his mind and looked for his first target.

He was already too late.

Two men were standing over him, their guns trained down on his chest.

Lincoln looked up into the face of a man he didn't recognize.

'Go on,' he muttered, 'shoot.'

'I will,' the man said, 'if you don't drop your gun.'

Lincoln was about to snap back a retort, but then his gaze alighted on the man's jacket and the star pinned there. He snorted an ironic laugh then dropped his gun and batted at his clothes to free himself of the last embers.

Then he coughed out a few rasping snorts of breath to clear his lungs before standing to face the lawman and, as he now saw, his deputy.

'Sheriff Cushing?' he asked.

'Sure. And you?'

'Marshal Lincoln Hawk. There's some associates of Keating Dobbs lying dead and unidentified in there.' He looked around, seeing no sign of Keating and the other men who had surrounded the building. 'As for Keating, he won't have gone far yet.'

Cushing narrowed his eyes. Then he

glanced at the deputy, who shrugged.

'The information that led you here is wrong, Marshal, but I'll be interested to see who you've got in there.' Cushing turned to the building, which was now fully ablaze. 'Provided there's anything left of them by the time we can get in.'

'There's no time to wait for that. Keating is getting away.' Lincoln headed off towards his horse while beckoning the lawmen to follow.

'We're not going on no wild chase,' Cushing shouted after him.

Lincoln stopped and turned back to see the lawmen hadn't moved.

'Why not?'

'Because we already have Keating Dobbs in a cell back in Utopia.' Cushing smiled. 'He gets hung tomorrow at sundown.'

3

'Is this supposed to be Keating Dobbs?' Lincoln asked, peering at the prisoner lying on his back on his cot.

'It is,' Sheriff Cushing said.

Lincoln considered the limited view of the prisoner's features he could see beneath the heavy bandages that coated his head, judging that he did resemble the man he had been close to apprehending.

'What's wrong with him?'

'He got shot. He's not come round.'

'Convenient,' Lincoln murmured, getting a hint of what had happened here. 'Who caught him and who confirmed he was Keating?'

'Richmond Cafferty.' Cushing raised a hand as Lincoln started to splutter. 'And before you cast aspersions, Richmond doesn't make mistakes.'

Lincoln gripped the bars as he

considered the situation, but no matter how he looked at it he could reach only one conclusion.

'I used to think that too,' he said.

When Lincoln turned from the cell it was to face the irate sheriff pointing a finger at him.

'I'm not standing for no US Marshal coming into my law office and telling me that Richmond Cafferty got it wrong. I've been sheriff here for nigh on fifteen years and this is the tenth man he's brought in.'

'I don't doubt his past record. I'm worried about his current one.' Lincoln considered the sheriff's flared eyes. 'And even if you're content, surely you wouldn't want an innocent man to get hung.'

Cushing shrugged. 'You want to prove that's not Keating, you need to do it real quick. We're hanging him tomorrow.'

'Why the hurry?'

'Because if we don't, he'll die and he's not escaping justice.'

Lincoln glanced into the cell. He judged that the comatose prisoner was unlikely to regain consciousness for long enough to work out what was happening to him.

'And then what happens,' he asked, 'when you later find out that you've hung the wrong man?'

'Then I'll find you and apologize for what I'm about to do.'

The sheriff cracked his knuckles while his deputy stood at his shoulder and set his feet wide apart in a belligerent stance.

Lincoln considered the truculent lawmen, then snorted a harsh laugh and backed away for a pace.

'There's no need for you to do something I'll make you regret.' Lincoln set off for the door. 'I'm leaving.'

He walked by the two lawmen, not catching their eyes.

'And don't ever come back here telling me that we're hanging the wrong man,' Cushing shouted after him.

Lincoln stopped in the doorway

looking into the road.

'When I return, I won't be telling you nothing because I'll be bringing you the right man.'

*   *   *

'Where have you been?' Cameron White asked.

'I've been making us rich,' Jack Miller said with a huge grin on his face. Then he beckoned Cameron to join him at the quieter end of the bar.

Cameron winced. 'You shouldn't be gambling with our money.'

'I wasn't doing no gambling. I was getting us the best deal you could ever imagine. You wouldn't have done any better. You'll be — '

Cameron laid a hand on Jack's shoulder to stop him babbling.

'Tell me one thing: how much of the money is left?'

'None, but — '

'You lost it all!'

'No.' Jack flinched back looking hurt.

'I invested it, like you said, and we'll double every cent within a year.'

Cameron sighed. 'What have you *invested* it in?'

'I bought us a saloon.'

Cameron took deep breaths to calm himself down. Then he looped an arm around his friend's shoulders while pointing at the door.

'Show me to our new saloon. Then I'll start working out how we can get our money back.'

Jack considered Cameron's stern expression.

'You'll change your mind when you see what I've bought.'

They headed to the door and, despite his sense of foreboding, Cameron hurried, hoping this would turn out well while still expecting that Jack had made a bad investment.

'Tell me what happened,' he asked when they were outside.

'I was looking for you and I went by the Chuck Wagon . . . our new saloon.' Jack pointed at a building on the edge of town. 'The owner, Gaston Prix, was outside, waiting to complete its sale. The buyer was late and the deal was to close at sundown, but then he saw me coming.'

'I reckon he probably did,' Cameron murmured, although from one hundred yards away the wooden building did appear impressive. 'Go on.'

'He'd already sold it for six hundred dollars, but I made him a higher offer. Gaston is a man of principle and he refused, but I haggled real good. Finally, just as the sun was about to set, I won him over with an offer of seven hundred and fifty dollars.'

Cameron continued to look at the saloon they were approaching, wondering how this deal would turn out to be a bad one, but the building still appeared sound.

'Did you see this other buyer?'

'I didn't.' Jack drew in his breath then removed a wad of papers from his pocket and slapped them into Cameron's hand. 'Read this. It's all as it appears.

We've got ourselves a saloon, and from what I could see from the outside, it looks mighty fine.'

'Is it his to sell?' Cameron said as he looked through the documents. He stopped and read the relevant details, but they all appeared to be in order. 'It does appear that Gaston was the owner.'

Jack grinned. 'I told you! I told you! I got us a great deal on the Chuck Wagon and you're too darned proud to admit it.'

Jack's proclamation made a passer-by look their way, then stop and come over.

'Are you two saying,' he asked, eyeing them with a gleam in his eye, 'that you've bought the Chuck Wagon?'

'We are,' Cameron said cautiously. 'Is there something wrong with that?'

The man snorted a laugh, then swung round and broke into a run, but he'd managed only two paces before Cameron took several long strides and grabbed his arm, halting him.

'Whoa there, stranger. What's the rush? I asked you a question. What's wrong with us buying Gaston Prix's saloon?'

The man struggled to escape, but finding that Cameron had a firm grip, he relented and swung round to face him. He was still smirking.

'Because Gaston's been trying to sell that *saloon* for the last five years to every fool with too much money and too little sense who's ridden into town. Except everyone's had the sense to ignore him . . . until now.'

'I knew it,' Cameron murmured. He released his grip, and before he could ask for more details, the man hurried off.

'Somebody's bought Gaston's saloon!' he cried out. 'Gaston's found two idiots to buy the Chuck Wagon!'

Cameron watched the man dart from side to side in the road shouting out the news and everyone he passed stopped him to ask for more details. Then they looked down the road at them. And they were all laughing.

'This don't look good,' Jack murmured.

'Maybe it won't be that bad,' Cameron said without much hope. 'Let's see what the problem is.'

They turned and, with his neck burning from the gazes of the mocking eyes, Cameron considered their property.

He now noted that the batwings were mouldering and that the doorway and windows were boarded up, but the false-fronted wooden wall had a sign proclaiming the saloon within, giving him hope that the situation may be salvageable.

With heavy treads they stepped up on to the boardwalk and stood before the door, considering how best to remove the boards.

Jack winced and turned away.

'I can't look,' he said, slapping a hand over his eyes. 'Tell me how bad it is.'

Cameron edged close to the boards blocking the doorway. He peered through a gap to see what lay beyond, and it wasn't a saloon. All that was there was a mouldering old chuck wagon lying on its side.

The building was nothing more than a propped-up false front.

'It's bad,' he said.

★   ★   ★

The trail had gone cold.

Lincoln slapped the ground in irritation then headed back into the draw, looking for the route his quarry had taken.

He had tracked Billy Maxwell through the day after Sheriff Griffith had carried through with his ultimatum and released him. Lincoln had figured that arresting him again would solve nothing when there was a mystery to clear up.

Billy had taken a straight and confident path that suggested he wasn't worried about being followed. Although where he might be heading was unclear as the only nearby settlement in this direction was the Mission San Juan.

On foot, Lincoln explored all the likely exits, but found no sign of where Billy had gone next.

Then a worrying thought hit him. If he couldn't find tracks that showed where Billy had gone, perhaps he was still here.

Lincoln chided himself for not having been cautious, then slipped into the scrub. He had hobbled his horse a half-mile back and he had to hope he hadn't been too noisy while he'd been searching.

Then he waited.

His view was of a hill that gently sloped away from him. Flat ground was on either side with scrub behind him, the undergrowth being dense enough to stop anyone sneaking up on him quietly.

Lincoln was a patient man and without difficulty he waited for Billy to show. But if Billy were in fact here, he was more patient than Lincoln expected. The sun disappeared behind the hill as the evening began with still no sign of him.

Twilight redness was lighting the sky when Lincoln resolved that he would await darkness before he accepted that Billy wasn't here, after all. But as the light level dropped a new source of light appeared.

At first it was just a brief glow beyond the hill that might have been a trick of the light. Then the glow flared highlighting the stark trees on the apex before disappearing.

'I've got you,' Lincoln murmured to himself in satisfaction.

He slipped out from the scrub and made his way up the hill to the side of the place where the glow had been.

The glow didn't appear again, but he presumed that Billy was guarding his fire, a theory that proved correct. On the other side of the hill the ground had fallen away and in the hollowed-out recess that was protected on three sides a lone man was sitting.

Lincoln crawled to the edge where he lay and watched him. The man's actions were relaxed as he moved around the fire and fiddled with a tin in which he was cooking something.

When the food was heated to his satisfaction he moved the stones around the fire and this flared the flames. Although the man had his head lowered, the increased light let him see the man's form.

To Lincoln's irritation he was slightly-built, which meant he wasn't Billy, but that irritation ended when the man raised his head.

'Keating Dobbs,' Lincoln whispered to himself, now delighted that his seemingly doomed quest had taken this unexpected but welcome twist.

He couldn't be sure why Keating was here, but it was a reasonable deduction that he was waiting to meet up with Billy. Lincoln also reckoned that Billy had realized that he was being followed and he had moved past the planned rendezvous point, aiming to put him off his trail.

Lincoln hoped that Billy would return when he was sure it was safe, so he didn't move in on Keating.

The first hint that his patience would be rewarded came when he saw movement against the night sky. He stared at that spot until he saw the movement again, confirming that a man was stealthily slipping towards the edge. At the edge the man looked at Keating, then settled down.

Lincoln wouldn't have expected Billy to arrive in a secretive way. So after watching the newcomer to confirm he wasn't going to let Keating know he'd arrived, Lincoln shuffled back from the edge and made his slow way around the recess towards him.

He stayed a few yards from the rim, as the ground that had fallen away was loose and he could easily dislodge dirt and alert Keating. At a cautious pace, Lincoln covered the thirty yards to the newcomer in ten minutes.

Five yards away from him he stopped, judging that he couldn't risk sneaking any closer without his quarry hearing him.

Then he watched the darkened profile of the man's face as he looked from Keating to the opening to the recess then back, as if he too was awaiting someone, presumably Billy.

Lincoln didn't have to wait long to be proved correct when a rider came into the firelight. Down below, Keating jumped to his feet, a gun in hand, but he relaxed when the rider hailed him.

'Put that gun down, Keating,' the newcomer said, 'it's me, Billy.'

'You're late,' Keating said.

'I took a detour. Someone was following me.'

Billy Maxwell got down from his horse then hunkered down beside the fire to warm his hands. He jabbed at the embers to gather a burst of flames, throwing the surroundings into stark relief.

Lincoln lowered himself as the light washed over him, but the other man didn't duck into hiding. Instead he stood, a movement that was sure to attract Keating's and Billy's attention.

When he was upright, he moved to the very edge, letting Lincoln see the man's face. Although he'd never met him before he was sure it was Richmond Cafferty, the bounty hunter who had made such a bad mistake about the men he'd handed over to justice in Pandora and Utopia.

Lincoln consoled himself with the thought that at least Richmond was attempting to rectify his mistake, even if he was about to do it in an incautious manner.

'Richmond?' he whispered.

The man turned at the hip while ducking then dropped to one knee to face Lincoln, although his darting eyes suggested he couldn't see him.

'It is,' he said, crawling away from the edge. 'Who's there?'

Richmond had spoken louder than Lincoln had, but down below Keating and Billy were chatting, masking his voice.

'Marshal Lincoln Hawk,' Lincoln whispered, while beckoning Richmond on. 'Explain yourself.'

Richmond's gaze centred in on Lincoln before he scurried along to join him.

'I tracked 'em,' Richmond said, glaring at him. 'I found 'em. I'll take 'em.'

'At least you've found the right men this time.' Lincoln sneered. 'But you didn't even know I was watching you, so I don't trust you enough to get anything else right. Now keep back while I deal with this.'

Richmond lowered his head, Lincoln's revelation making him shame-faced. He backed away for a pace, but as he was close to the edge his movement dislodged several stones.

The outlaws below didn't notice them, but the shifting stones heralded an even worse problem. Without warning, a stretch of ground several yards wide slipped away beneath Richmond's feet and dropped him to his chest.

As the rumbling dirt cascaded down the slope, both outlaws leapt to their feet to look up. They were faced with the sight of Richmond's legs dangling over the edge with his feet wheeling and struggling to find purchase.

'Who's up there?' Keating shouted.

Now unable to move in on the outlaws unseen, Lincoln lunged for Richmond's waving arms, but then the unequal battle between gravity and Richmond's attempts to find traction reached its inevitable conclusion.

In a vast plume of dust, he rolled away while kicking out his arms and legs trying to stop his progress.

Then the gunfire started.

A rapid volley of gunshots ripped along the top of the recess, forcing Lincoln to drop from view. He waited until the volley had petered out then looked over the edge, but it was to see that Keating and Billy had already reached their horses.

Richmond was lying on his chest at the bottom of the recess, his form unmoving after having been, presumably, shot. Lincoln reckoned that was no less than he deserved for his incompetence.

He got a bead on the nearest outlaw and tore off a couple of wild shots, but by then Keating and Billy were thundering away into the darkness.

As Billy returned a volley of high slugs, Lincoln took careful aim and blasted a gunshot, but it only tore a hole in Billy's hat. Then he and Keating galloped off into the night.

Lincoln still fired wildly in the direction they'd gone to work off his irritation. Then he sat down and muttered a few choice curses.

It'd take him a while to get back to his horse. By the time he'd returned, the outlaws would be long gone, and pursuing them in the dark would probably prove to be a fruitless exercise.

Resigned now to the fact that he wouldn't be able to pick up their trail until first light Lincoln slid down the slope to check on Richmond.

When he reached the bottom he found that the bounty hunter hadn't been shot, after all. Richmond was stirring and rubbing his head. So Lincoln hunkered down beside him.

'You fine?' he asked.

'I will be when I've caught my breath,' Richmond said.

'But you won't be after I've finished with you.'

Richmond glanced at the entrance then winced.

'That mean they got away?'

'No. Your stupidity alerted them and let them escape.'

'I slipped,' Richmond murmured, although he didn't meet his eye. 'It was an accident.'

Lincoln knew Richmond only through his reputation, but everything he'd heard about him appeared to be wrong. The fearless hunter who had tracked down over a hundred outlaws and who for over twenty years had never failed to get the man he was after was just a wizened old man.

Worse, he was uncertain and meek.

'What happened to you?' Lincoln asked.

Richmond looked up, his abashed expression showing he'd picked up on Lincoln's thoughts.

'I got old.'

Lincoln had been ready to berate Richmond, but this admittance made him move round to sit beside him.

'It comes to everyone,' he said. 'Admitting that might make sure you don't go a-rolling and a-hollering into an outlaws' campsite again.'

Richmond provided a rueful smile. 'I made a mess of that, but believe me when I say this: I will put it right.'

'You can't. There's a dead man in Pandora who everyone thinks is Billy Maxwell and there's another man will have been hanged by now in Utopia for being Keating Dobbs.'

'That's not as bad as it sounds. Nobody suffered.' Richmond sat up and sighed as he recalled the events. 'I'd been tracking Billy when I came

46

across two men shooting each other up. They both died, but one of the men looked like Billy. So I reckoned I'd had a stroke of luck and took his body in.'

Lincoln conceded this explanation with a shrug.

'And the man you said was Keating Dobbs?'

'I did take advantage there. This man killed his brother up in Jackson County then ran. I put off finding Keating to drag him in, but he put up one hell of a fight. I shot him and took him to Utopia. He was half-dead but Sheriff Cushing decided it was Keating Dobbs.' Richmond frowned and cast a glance at Lincoln. 'I didn't put him right.'

'Why the deception?'

'It's . . . it's mighty hard for me.' Richmond looked at his hands, considering the slight tremor there. 'Every day I lose a bit more of the man I was, but I still have a reputation to keep up.'

'Which will take one hell of a pounding when outlaws you claimed to have caught commit new crimes.'

'I know that.' Richmond slapped his holster. 'I was putting that right when you sneaked up on me.'

'You were putting nothing right. If I hadn't have come along, they'd have killed you. You were standing up, making noise . . . ' Lincoln waved his arms in exasperation as he struggled to remember all the things Richmond had done wrong. 'It's time for you to give up before people die in the name of you keeping your reputation.'

'I did wrong.' Richmond flashed Lincoln a hopeful smile. 'If you say I shouldn't do this on my own, I won't, but let me help you.'

'You're doing nothing but hanging up your gun.' Lincoln glared at Richmond until he lowered his head, then softened his tone. 'When I bring in Keating and Billy I won't tell anyone what I've learnt here. Questions will be raised, but your reputation should just about survive. But if you continue with your bumbling attempts to catch outlaws, I'll let everyone know what you've become.'

Richmond hunched his shoulders, seeming to shrink before Lincoln's eyes.

'I'll retire,' he murmured finally.

'Just see that you do,' Lincoln said with relief.

Then without further comment he turned his back on the old bounty hunter and headed away.

4

'Gaston Prix?' Cameron White asked, stepping into the light.

The man who had been hunched over the fire warming his hands looked up, a hand straying to his holster.

'I have never heard of him,' he said.

Cameron snorted a laugh as he got the response he'd expected.

Finding Gaston hadn't been too hard. Everyone in town had wanted to talk about him, especially when they'd learnt that for once his tall tales had worked and made him a lot of money.

Apparently Gaston was an irrepressible rogue who was always dreaming up moneymaking schemes, this being one of the few to have worked, a revelation that didn't help Cameron's and Jack's already dour moods.

They had been directed to a ramshackle building nestling beside a creek ten miles out of town. Gaston hadn't been there but they'd been assured he would return.

After a few hours of waiting, their patience had been rewarded. They had given him enough time to settle down and become off guard. When he'd started roasting a fish on a fire outside, they'd made their move.

'You're saying that you live here and yet you've never heard of Gaston Prix,' Cameron said, 'the most infamous man in town.'

'I stay out of town. I trust nobody there.'

Cameron laughed loudly, ensuring he had Gaston's attention so that he didn't hear Jack making his way around the house behind him.

Gaston's hand was moving closer to his gun when Jack appeared, his gun already drawn and aimed at Gaston's back.

'Raise that hand,' he said.

'I have nothing to steal. I am a poor man. I am . . . ' Gaston trailed off when

Jack moved into his line of sight. He sneered. 'I am a man who doesn't give refunds.'

'Then you can make an exception,' Jack said. 'I've decided I don't want to be a saloon owner, seeing as how the saloon you sold me needs some work done on it before I can serve customers.'

'Like getting some walls,' Cameron said.

'And a roof,' Jack added.

Gaston licked his lips as he looked from one man to the other.

'I'd like to oblige, but I've had that building for many years and — '

'You're not listening,' Jack snapped. 'We want our money back and we're not leaving without it, one way or the other.'

Gaston gulped. 'And you're not listening. You can't have your money back. I don't have it any more.'

Cameron narrowed his eyes. 'You can't have spent it already. Jack only gave you the money yesterday.'

'I didn't spend it,' Gaston murmured, lowering his head, his tone sounding honest. 'The news got out that I had money. So every person I owed came out of hiding for a share of my windfall. I've only got about twenty dollars left.'

As Gaston reached into his pocket and withdrew a few bills, Jack looked at Cameron.

'Do we believe this story?' he asked.

Cameron maintained his stern expression for several seconds. Then with a sigh he hunkered down on the other side of the fire.

In reality, he didn't have the stomach for getting their money back by roughing up Gaston, but he had hoped they might worry him into handing it over.

Cameron held out his hand and Gaston passed over the bills. He rooted through them to confirm they amounted to eighteen dollars. He laughed.

'Last week we had twenty dollars between us. Then we won a heap of money. Then we lost it. Now we have about twenty dollars again. This hasn't been the first time and I guess it won't be the last.'

Jack hunkered down beside Cameron to warm his hands.

'I guess it won't,' he said.

Gaston glanced at one man then the other, his wide eyes registering his surprise at their sudden change in attitude.

'So you two are like me, then?' he asked cautiously. 'Sometimes you get lucky, more often you don't, but that doesn't stop you seeking out golden opportunities to get rich?'

'In many ways we're like you,' Jack said, smiling before he firmed his expression. 'Except we're honest men looking for honest work.'

'And all we've got is the money you gave us,' Cameron said, reckoning that the irrepressible Gaston was laying another trap to steal even the small amount of money they had left. 'And you're not having that.'

'I don't want it,' Gaston said. 'I have an idea in mind that'll make you thousands of dollars.'

Jack snorted. 'You said that about the Chuck Wagon.'

'But this time, it's for real.' Gaston leaned forward. 'Have you heard of the legend of the Mission San Juan?'

'Nope,' Cameron snapped with determination, 'and we're not listening to no more tall tales.'

'This is no tall tale.' Gaston gestured at the fire, inviting them to stay. 'And it'll cost you nothing to hear it.'

Cameron winced. 'Those are the kind of tales that worry me the most.'

★ ★ ★

Richmond Cafferty sat beside the dying fire that Keating Dobbs had lit earlier.

Lincoln had left some hours ago and he was now sure he wouldn't return, but even so he sat pensively looking into the flames.

At his side was a bottle of whiskey he'd taken from his saddle-bag, but it remained unopened as he pondered.

The lawman's contempt for him had affected him more than he'd thought it would, and even then Lincoln hadn't known the full details of everything he'd done. So he sat quietly, unwilling to take the next step.

Perhaps some part of the man he'd been told him to do nothing and let fate decide his future. If nobody sought him out, he could move on with his reputation suffering only minor tarnishing. Only if others decreed it would he have to complete what he'd started.

It was long after midnight and he'd heard nothing but animal sounds when he got the first hint that something was amiss. A horse snickered close by. Then he caught movement from beyond the opening to the recess.

He moved from the fire and peered into the darkness.

'Lincoln?' he asked.

Silence greeted him although again he saw movement and this time he was sure that more than one form was approaching him.

He drew his gun. Then he backed into the furthest corner of the recess where the steep walls provided him with some cover.

For several minutes he waited for whoever was out there to come for him, but when they did, they came openly.

Keating Dobbs stepped into view in the entrance; Billy Maxwell joined him five paces to his side. Then in the space between them a third man appeared from the gloom. With slow deliberate paces he went through the gap, keeping his face lowered.

Ten paces from the fire the man stopped. The outlaws moved on to flank him. Slowly the man raised his head. The flickering light played across his hard-boned face, showing Richmond that he was Lawrence Shannon.

'So,' Richmond said with a pronounced gulp, 'the Lawrence Shannon gang have joined up again.'

'We had to,' Lawrence said, smiling, his teeth bright in the firelight, 'when we have unfinished business.'

5

'It's smaller than I expected,' Cameron said.

'And more decrepit,' Jack said.

Gaston laughed. 'The Mission San Juan has seen many battles. It's a wonder it's still standing.'

'Then before it falls down,' Cameron said, 'show us this wonder that'll make us rich men.'

Gaston nodded then rode on towards the main gateway.

The mission was two hundred years old. Originally built by the Spanish it had prospered and had grown to create a settlement that had supported hundreds of people. But fifty years ago repeated assaults first by Comanche raiders and then bandits had destroyed the settlement, the padres had left, and the mission had been abandoned to decay and neglect.

Twenty years ago the Quintos family had taken over the buildings and now it supported life again, and more than just their family. Through the open gateway Cameron saw people milling around and in the rude adobe buildings outside people had set up residence.

Despite these signs of life, they rode past the settlement without anyone paying them any attention then into the mission itself. Within the walls, one-storey buildings were set out around the quadrangle, many lacking roofs and each with crumbling walls. However, one building by the far wall had had new timbers erected to create a sheltered area, suggesting some rebuilding was underway.

The most impressive building was the chapel. When they'd left their horses in the stable they saw that a wide-open door led into an interior that was bright and welcoming, and above the door there was an impressive eighty-foot-high bell tower.

Gaston glanced at the lowering sun,

then beckoned for them to take up a position opposite the chapel against the perimeter wall.

'Now,' he said, 'we wait.'

Jack glanced at Cameron, his raised eyebrows questioning whether they should ask for more information, but Cameron shrugged, deciding to let Gaston explain in his own good time. They settled down.

An hour passed quietly. Then gradually people gravitated into the quadrangle. Cameron presumed they came from the settlement outside. All of them were either elderly or infirm.

Presently, six padres dressed in cassocks emerged from the new timber building. They walked in a line to the chapel. Four filed inside, while two men stayed outside and beckoned to the gathering with brief gestures.

This was the cue for the people to make their way over to the chapel and form an orderly queue. Cameron and Jack moved to join them, but Gaston held them back, signifying that they should file in at the rear.

They waited until half the gathered people had disappeared from view and it appeared that nobody else would join the queue. Then Gaston indicated that they should move off.

He had been smiling as he watched the proceedings, but he held his hands before his face and when he removed them, the smile had gone. Then he hunched his shoulders and moved off.

Cameron and Jack walked beside him, matching the pace of his slow and stumbling gait. Slowly Gaston looked at each of them then shook his head.

'You're poor, downtrodden and hungry,' he said from the corner of his mouth. Then he winked. 'So look it!'

With sighs, Cameron and Jack matched his slouching posture and desperate expression. Their new demeanour received a supportive nod before they headed on to the chapel.

When they arrived, they tagged on behind the last few to enter and listened to the brief conversation the padres at the door had with each entrant.

'Bless you, my son,' one padre said.

'Bless you, Father,' the entrant said before slipping through the door and letting the next man take his position.

This simple process continued until Gaston stepped forward.

'Bless — ' The padre winced, then snapped up to an upright position and replaced his previous hushed tones with a normal speaking voice. 'So, Gaston Prix is back again!'

'I am tired and hungry and in need of spiritual salvation, Father Bartholomew,' Gaston said, still maintaining his downtrodden expression.

'If ever there was someone in need of salvation, it's you. And for that reason you are always welcome here.' Father Bartholomew provided a beatific smile, but when Gaston moved to enter, he shot out a hand and took his arm. 'But remember that when you leave, the food is for everyone, the relics stay here, and most importantly: we have no gold.'

'I understand, Father.' Gaston gestured with a vague movement that might have been an attempt to form a cross on his chest before he shuffled into the chapel.

Cameron stepped up next and smiled.

'We're not with him,' he said.

'Then bless you. You are always welcome at the Mission San Juan.'

Then the padre moved on to welcome Jack.

Once inside, Cameron looked around the chapel, noting its simple interior. There were several pews, now being filled, and behind the altar at the front of the chapel a long red curtain had been drawn across to cut off the view of the presbytery beyond.

There were also signs of the past troubles, with many holes, presumably gunshots, in the walls, and around the door the walls were sooty and charred. There was no smell of burning so Cameron reckoned the fire had happened some time ago.

When he looked up, he saw shortened

burnt planks set into the wall at regular intervals. This made him think that steps had been here, presumably leading to the bell tower, but which had now burnt down.

He pointed this out to Jack who agreed with his assessment, although when he mentioned it to Gaston, he urged him to be quiet as Bartholomew was about to start the service.

So they sat on a pew at the back and for the next half-hour they bided away their time through a simple religious ceremony.

In Cameron's view the rest of the congregation weren't too interested in the ceremony either. Food had been laid out on the altar and most of the people's gazes were set on that rather than Bartholomew.

Accordingly, the moment the service ended and Bartholomew asked everyone to join him at the front, Cameron expected that there would be a rush to eat, but instead two padres drew back the curtain.

In the revealed space behind the altar there was a statue of a supine man on a stone block, the sight making Gaston shuffle on his pew. Against each wall and facing the statue, two men stood. Both men wore formal red uniforms that made them appear to be guards.

'What's this?' Cameron whispered, leaning towards Gaston.

'This,' Gaston said, 'is what I brought you here to see: the statute of Saint John, the Soldier Saint.'

'A statue!' Jack muttered. 'Why?'

Gaston chuckled. 'Because, my two impatient friends, he will give us more gold than you could ever dream of owning.'

⋆ ⋆ ⋆

Lincoln fingered the whiskey glass as he hunched over the bar and pondered on his next actions.

Keating Dobbs and Billy Maxwell had covered their tracks well, leaving him with no direction to follow. So he had returned to Utopia to see if anyone had heard any news, but with the man Sheriff Cushing believed to be Keating having been hanged yesterday, nobody had.

Now his only option was to back hunches, but in truth he didn't hold out much hope of locating them until the inevitable happened and they returned to their old ways.

He was still annoyed about Richmond Cafferty's behaviour, so when Richmond entered the bar he gripped his hand into a fist so tightly he was in danger of breaking the glass.

On seeing Lincoln, Richmond stopped a pace in from the door.

The two men glared at each other. Then with a shrug and not meeting Lincoln's eye Richmond headed to the opposite end of the bar where he hunched over in a deliberate show of not looking Lincoln's way.

They stayed that way until with a muttered comment to himself and a roll of the shoulders Richmond edged down the bar to stand beside Lincoln.

'As we'll probably keep on crossing paths,' Richmond said with a resigned sigh, 'we can't ignore each other.'

'Ignoring is fine with me,' Lincoln said staring straight ahead, 'seeing as how we've not got nothing to say to each other.'

Richmond nodded. He threw whiskey down his throat with a determined motion that suggested he was seeking courage then refilled the glass.

'But I have something to say. I was wrong and I'm grateful you haven't told anyone about what I did. Whether you want it or not, you've got a friend here and if there's anything I can ever do for you, just ask.'

Lincoln firmed his jaw. He was minded to say nothing and wait for Richmond to leave, but the bounty hunter continued to look at him.

'Obliged for the sentiment,' Lincoln said finally, 'but the only thing I want of you is that you retire.'

Richmond sighed, raised his glass to

his lips, then lowered it without drinking and sighed again. His demeanour suggested that something was on his mind and that he was wondering whether he should voice it, but Lincoln didn't feel inclined to encourage him.

'In that case,' Richmond said, 'you'd better have this.'

Richmond placed a hand on the bar then slid it towards Lincoln's hand. He glanced around the saloon to check that nobody was looking their way, then raised the hand for a brief moment letting Lincoln catch a flash of gold.

Richmond kept his hand over the object until Lincoln gestured to an unoccupied table in a quiet corner of the saloon.

'All right,' Lincoln said when Richmond joined him, 'what you got there?'

'Maybe a clue as to how you can bring Lawrence Shannon and the other two to justice.'

Richmond placed a shielded fist on the table then opened his hand to let

Lincoln see that he was holding a coin.

When Richmond let him take it, Lincoln slipped the coin beneath the table to examine it more closely. The coin had an intricate design on one side and a stern-looking bust on the other. He couldn't decipher the wording other than the date of '1821' and the number '8' on the other side.

'Mexican?' he guessed.

Richmond nodded. 'An eight escudo coin and nearly an ounce of pure gold.'

'Where did you get it?'

'It's a long story and I don't reckon you want to hear about any more of my exploits, but let's just say I found it back in the draw. That level of carelessness means only one thing to me.'

'They could afford to lose it.'

Richmond nodded. 'And, as there's been no reports of gold going missing, that means they're planning to get their hands on a whole heap more.'

Lincoln considered the smile playing at the corners of Richmond's lips.

'And you reckon you know where they can get them?'

Richmond leaned towards him. 'Someone who lives nearby was once famed for paying with coins such as these. He's gravely ill now but still, there is a rumour, one that has been repeated so many times it has become legend, that he still has many more.'

'If this rumour is that well known I can easily find out who, so stop stringing this story along.'

'You can find out, but I want to join you. I made a mistake and I need to put that right. If we join forces, we can get all three outlaws when they join up to steal the gold.'

Lincoln rolled the coin over in his hand, feeling its coldness, then considered Richmond's hopeful look.

'All right,' he said, handing him back the coin. 'I'll accept your help, but you'll follow my orders and no matter whether we're successful or not, this will be your last time on the owlhoot trail.'

'I can't think of a better way to end it, but this won't be a long trail. They'll be interested in a place twenty miles out of town.' Richmond pocketed the gold coin. 'The owner of the gold is José Quintos from the Mission San Juan.'

6

Cameron watched the people in front of him in the chapel edge forward. They craned their necks to see what was happening before the altar while the padres began a keening chant that echoed high above them.

Two men on the front pew stood and made their way past the altar to the statue.

One man was around Cameron's age, the other old and hunched over and he had to be guided by the younger man. They went to the side of the stone block where they stood with their hands clasped before them.

With everyone nudging forward, Cameron joined them. Closer to, he saw that the statue must once have been impressive. It depicted a supine man with his hands clasped over his chest. Many gouges had been hewn from his form; the worst being a deep cut across the face and a missing upper arm.

He also discerned what the padres were chanting.

'San Juan,' they sang. 'San Juan.'

The old man lent forward and brushed a kiss against a ring that had been wedged between two fingers of the statue's hand. At that moment the chanting grew in volume and continued for a dozen cries of his name. Then the chant cut off.

With a nod to the statue the old man turned and walked away. The act of kissing the ring appeared to have given him strength and he walked unaided to the door at the back of the chapel.

The younger man followed with his arms spread wide in a way that made it look as if he expected the older man to stumble. But he carried on until he reached the door where he came to a halt and swirled round.

'The bell?' he asked, his voice high-pitched and echoing in the chapel.

'Can I sound the bell?'

'No, Father,' the younger man said, laying a gentle hand on his shoulder. 'Not today.'

'But, Francisco, it's sundown and I always sound the bell at sundown.' He looked around eagerly.

'Not any more you don't,' Francisco said, his strained voice betraying his tenseness, suggesting they'd had this conversation many times. 'Please try to remember. It's been many years since the bell stopped ringing. The steps have gone and — '

'But I want to ring it.' The old man tried to push Francisco aside and make a run into the main body of the chapel, but Francisco held on to him, then drew him to his chest.

They stood in that manner for a while with the old man murmuring to himself until he gave up fighting and let his son take him to the door. He was now shaking, the strength that the ceremony with the statue had provided having deserted him.

After both men had left, silence reigned for a minute.

Then the guards drew the curtain back across the chapel, cutting the statue off from view, while Father Bartholomew encouraged everyone to approach the altar. In an orderly fashion the padres then handed out the food and water.

With Gaston not explaining what they'd seen, Cameron joined the queue. Only when he and Jack had been given their share and they were heading outside to eat did he ask for an explanation.

'Who were the two men?' he asked. 'And what was that ceremony?'

'And where,' Jack said, leaning over, 'is this gold you bought us here to find?'

By way of a response Gaston smiled and nodded ahead, signifying they would speak when they were somewhere quieter.

Outside, most of the people who had been provided with food returned to their homes while the rest mingled against the sheltering perimeter wall opposite the chapel. Gaston picked a spot away from the bulk of them.

'That ceremony takes place every sundown,' he said. He bit off and chewed a corner of bread. 'Francisco Quintos and his father José leave their house behind the chapel and join the other pilgrims. José kisses his dead wife's ring that is now in the statue's safekeeping because Father Bartholomew has convinced his son that faith and all that nonsense will make him regain his mind and stop ranting on about the bell.'

'But it's not working?'

'I doubt anything will. Tonight he was calmer than the last time I saw him, but that's only because he's growing weaker.' Gaston sighed and when he continued his voice was sad, as if the events he described genuinely moved him. 'José had taken this abandoned mission as a home, but ten years ago bandits ransacked the place in search of the gold. They killed his wife and the ordeal he suffered stole his mind, but he didn't tell them where it was.'

'And that's the gold we're here to find?'

'It is.' Gaston leaned forward and smirked. 'And I know how to get it.'

'You mean steal it?'

'What else could I mean?'

Cameron stared at him then at Jack, who returned an angry shake of the head.

'You told us,' Jack said, 'that nobody would suffer from us finding the gold.'

'And nobody will. Francisco isn't using it and when he and José die it'll just go to the Church and — '

'We're not interested.'

Gaston looked at each man in turn, appraising their firm head shakes and folded arms.

'But you're the same as I am, looking for that one golden chance to get rich.'

'We are, and we'll probably never find it, but that doesn't matter. We've never stolen, never harmed anyone. So we're not stealing from those unfortunate men and from these padres who are helping the poor and the destitute.'

Gaston shrugged. 'I don't understand.'

'I know,' Jack said, stepping forward to loom over Gaston, 'and that's why we're parting company and why we don't ever want to see or hear of you or your ill-judged plans again.'

Jack glanced down at his gun with a significant gesture that warned Gaston about what would happen if they did meet again.

Gaston pouted, looking as if he'd argue with them, but then he sloped off to take up a position beside the wall on his own.

It was now fully dark and the padres were going round those who had stayed in the mission handing out blankets. After a brief consultation, Cameron and Jack decided that after they'd finished eating they'd rest here for the night.

'At least we won't have to spend any

more time with him,' Cameron said.

'I know, but everyone still thinks we're with him.' Jack pointed at the gateway where one of the guards had come outside to watch them. 'People have been watching us ever since we arrived.'

Cameron looked at the guard then around the perimeter of the mission. He saw that a second guard was loitering near the stables and he too was looking at them. Then he looked to where Gaston had gone to sit, but he'd scurried off into hiding somewhere.

'And they're not interested in Gaston, wherever he's gone. They probably reckon they can deal with him, but we're an unknown threat.'

Jack sighed. 'We should never have got involved with him. We leave as soon as we can tomorrow and we don't look back.'

'Agreed,' Cameron said as a padre joined them, 'but there's one thing we need to do first.'

Cameron said nothing more as the

padre handed them blankets, but when he turned to go, he raised a hand, halting him.

'Is anything troubling you?' the padre, who had identified himself as Father Raphael, asked.

'Yes,' Cameron said. 'It's that man who came in with us.'

Raphael provided an understanding smile.

'Gaston Prix is a troubled soul. But no matter how many times he disappoints, we will always welcome him back.'

'But perhaps not this time. He's planning to steal the gold that . . . ' Cameron trailed off when Raphael uttered a peel of laughter.

'Gaston is *always* planning to steal the gold. He's tried everything to find it: climbing over every wall in the mission, digging under the chapel. He is most persistent, an admirable trait in those as troubled as Gaston is.'

'And he's still persistent. He sounded sure he could get hold of it this time.'

Raphael maintained a sympathetic smile as he considered them, then offered a resigned sigh.

'If it will put your mind at rest, I will find him then sit with him tonight and read him a favourite scripture. That will dissuade him.' When Cameron started to say this wouldn't work Raphael winked. 'And if not, it'll ensure he doesn't have the freedom to cause any mischief.'

'That would be wise,' Cameron said, smiling.

Raphael moved to go, but before he left, another padre came running over from the chapel, demonstrating more haste than Cameron had seen anyone else here show.

'Father Raphael,' the man said. 'You need to come. We have a problem.'

'Gaston,' Cameron murmured, and despite Raphael's willingness to see the good in everyone the forlorn look he gave him said he thought this to be the case, too.

They headed to the chapel and on

entering Cameron saw that the red curtain behind the altar had been drawn back. Father Bartholomew was standing beside the statue. Consternation made him wring his hands.

Behind the statue a guard held a hand to his forehead and had adopted a hunched stance that registered a strong emotion, perhaps annoyance, perhaps even fear, as he cast concerned looks at the two burly padres who flanked him.

With an angry gesture Bartholomew beckoned Raphael on.

'What do you make of this?' he said, pointing at the statue.

Raphael approached with due solemnity and cast a sorrowful look along the length of the statue. He flinched, then looked at Bartholomew.

'The ring has gone,' he murmured aghast.

'To be precise, the ring has been stolen.'

'This is unfortunate, but we will find it. I have faith in the honesty of the good pilgrims who come to the mission. Someone will know who did it.'

'I already do.' Bartholomew held out a sheet of paper. 'Gaston Prix left this demand.'

Raphael read the offered paper then handed it back.

'Gaston is a familiar visitor. We will find him.'

'See that you do.' Bartholomew bowed, dismissing Raphael, who returned the bow then traipsed off to the door.

Cameron and Jack moved to follow him, but Bartholomew bade them to stay.

'We weren't friends of Gaston,' Cameron said. 'We don't know where he is.'

'Gaston has no friends and I accept it's unlikely you were a willing part of his plan.' Bartholomew glanced at the disgraced guard. 'Gaston has tried many times to steal from us, but his arrival with two new faces meant the guards spent more time watching you than him, and that provided a distraction for him to act.'

'He used us,' Jack murmured forlornly.

'He did,' Cameron said, 'but he was interested in gold not a ring.'

Bartholomew waved the paper Gaston had left.

'According to his demand he is still interested in gold.' Bartholomew read from the paper. ''Give me the gold by sundown tomorrow and I will return the ring.''

Cameron shrugged, not seeing why such a threat had caused so much consternation.

'Why is the ring important?' he asked.

'Because every day at sundown, José comes here to kiss his deceased wife's ring. It is the only comfort that poor man enjoys.'

'And what will he do if the ring isn't there for him to kiss?'

Bartholomew placed a firm hand on Cameron's right shoulder.

'He will probably lose his last tenuous hold on sanity and his son will deem the arrangement we have operated over. All he asked of me was that I treated José with respect. And I have, but now Gaston has finally found my weakness and all that I have built here is at risk.'

Bartholomew gestured around the chapel, inviting Cameron to follow his gaze. Aside from the two padres who were flanking the guard, there was little to see, but Cameron gathered that a compliment wouldn't go amiss.

'This is an impressive place. You administer to those in need without question, and that is very worthy.'

'It is. With Francisco's help I have begun to rebuild, and one day this mission will again be everything it once was: the centre of a community devoted to our Lord. I will ensure that nothing comes in the way of that aim.'

Bartholomew removed his hand and backed away for a pace. He slipped his hands into the cuffs of his cassock so that they disappeared from view then gave a brief nod to the two burly padres.

These men stepped up behind Cameron and Jack, presumably to shepherd them away now that their meeting was over. But then a pile-driver of a punch thudded into Cameron's kidneys making him drop to his knees.

A second punch sounded as Jack received the same treatment.

Cameron looked up at Bartholomew, expecting he would be shocked, but he said nothing as a swiped blow with two bunched fists to the side of the head sent Cameron reeling to lie prostrate.

His senses swirled as he heard Jack fight back. Slaps and punches sounded, followed by Jack's cry of pain. Then the sound of a body hitting the floor echoed.

For long moments there was silence. Then Bartholomew grabbed Cameron's hair and raised his head.

'You didn't need to hurt us,'

Cameron murmured. 'We were going to help you.'

'I am pleased to hear it, but the Lord's way is sometimes a painful way and I have found that a demonstration often concentrates the minds of deviant novices.' Bartholomew leaned down to place his face a few inches from Cameron's. 'Do you know of the history of our blessed saints?'

'No.'

'A pity. Many of them suffered terrible slow deaths, but their reward was sainthood.' Bartholomew offered a cold thin smile. 'If San Juan isn't clasping the ring come sundown tomorrow, know this: you'll get to suffer their torment without the reward of sainthood.'

7

'We'll hole up on the outcrop,' Richmond Cafferty said. 'It has the best view of the mission we can get.'

Lincoln considered the boulder-strewn outcrop. It was situated a mile from the mission so he accepted it was a good place to stop, but he still shook his head.

'We carry on to the mission,' he said. 'I want to find out the truth about this gold.'

Richmond snorted. 'Nobody has got to the truth about José Quintos's gold. Not even the bandits who raided the place ten years ago and took his mind found out. His son won't turn his back on a lifetime of silence and talk to you.'

'Then this all could be for nothing?'

'It could. There might be gold, there might not be. All that matters is that Lawrence Shannon believes the gold is there. And if he comes, from here we'll be able to see him.'

Lincoln rubbed his jaw while he considered, then gave a curt nod. So they dismounted and found positions within the rocks at a high point where they could see in all directions.

The sun was poking out from behind the distant mountains when they settled down for what could be a long wait.

Although holing up here was preferable to riding around following trails that led nowhere, not knowing when or even if Lawrence Shannon would come meant it wouldn't be a restful wait.

The fact that he had few reasons to trust Richmond's hunch didn't help either. But he had no better plan in mind and so he settled down twenty yards from Richmond.

He looked at the mission while Richmond looked the other way.

As the sun rose, people emerged from the buildings outside the mission walls, and within the walls other people headed into the chapel.

'Stop worrying about the mission,' Richmond said, 'come and see this.'

With the mission being a centre of activity, Lincoln expected that they would be watching people come and go all day, but to his surprise when he joined Richmond, the three riders who were approaching appeared promising.

'That's surely not Lawrence coming already,' Lincoln said, struggling to discern the distant figures. 'We've only been here for an hour.'

'Sometimes you get lucky,' Richmond said while squinting at the men, who were now a quarter-mile away. 'And today we have. Those men are Lawrence Shannon, Keating Dobbs and Billy Maxwell.'

Lincoln nodded, the men now being close enough for him to recognize them.

'And,' he said, 'they're heading here.'

Richmond smiled. 'I told you this was the best place to hole up and watch the mission.'

'One success doesn't make up for all

the mistakes you've made. Now wait until they get closer and we'll blast 'em to hell.'

'That's risky. I know this outcrop and they can go to ground in an instant. We need to use the element of surprise to full effect.' Richmond pointed at the highest point of the jumble of rocks. 'I'll head there and pin them down while you go down to ground level and outflank them.'

Lincoln wasn't used to being given orders, but even though Richmond was giving them, he had to bow to his superior knowledge of the area.

'All right,' he said. 'We split up.'

Richmond nodded. Then he made his cautious way over to the large boulder he had indicated.

Lincoln watched his progress until he was sure of the position he was taking up. By now, the three outlaws were 200 yards from the rocks and were looking around as they picked the best position to head for.

Lincoln waited until Lawrence pointed

at a gap between two boulders fifty feet to his side. Then, on the opposite side of the outcrop to the outlaws, he hurried down to ground level, bounding from rock to rock.

When he reached the ground he skirted around the edge of the boulders, only slowing when the other side came into view. He had been fast enough to come out while the outlaws were still riding. So he stopped beside the final boulder and watched them dismount.

He took a bead on Lawrence Shannon and waited until he had a clear shot. But Lawrence darted around as he looked along the outcrop, picking his route to the top, making the shot difficult.

Worse, the other two men remained out of view, being hidden by their horses as they led them to the bottom of the outcrop.

Lincoln gritted his teeth in irritation, judging that Richmond had made a mistake in his plan to outflank them rather than just remain in hiding.

His irritation grew when he saw movement on the high rock. Richmond appeared and gave a gesture across his throat then a raised hand before he slipped back into hiding.

Lincoln sighed, noting that here again was proof that the bounty hunter had lost his touch. But despite Richmond's reckless action in giving Lincoln an unnecessary message, Lawrence showed no sign that he'd seen it as he pointed up the slope.

Then the three men made their way on foot up towards the gap. It was a steep climb and so they went in single file with Billy leading.

At the rear Lawrence provided cover, although from his position the plains were devoid of life. When Billy reached the top he took on the covering duties while Lawrence and Keating climbed up.

Accordingly, Lincoln waited until all three men reached the gap and disappeared from view. Then while keeping his back to the rock, he worked his way around the boulder and then along the base of the outcrop, taking a route where he couldn't see the top.

He stopped at the point where the outlaws had climbed. He judged that following their route would be a risky action, as the terrain was open, but he couldn't see that he had a choice.

Then he saw movement on the high rock.

Richmond gave him a shooing gesture then a thumbs-up signal. This second reckless act made Lincoln consider returning a gesture of his own. But as from his position Richmond would be able to see that the route was clear, he bit back his irritation and moved on.

Lincoln climbed while looking at the gap above him and the boulders on either side. Ten yards from cresting the top he dropped to his knees and then, eight yards later, to his belly.

When he peered over the crest between the two flanking boulders,

Lawrence was lying on flat rock five yards away with his back to him, peering at the mission.

A rifle, water bottle and other equipment was lying scattered along the extent of the rock, suggesting that although Billy and Keating were out of view they were on either side of him.

He wormed forward, coming to the edge of the boulders, making every movement with extreme slowness, and, as he'd hoped, Billy and then Keating came into view.

They were watching the mission with rapt concentration. They were also in clear view from the high rock. From fifty yards away Richmond might not be accurate with all of his gunfire, but he should be able to decimate them.

He planted his elbows wide apart, settled himself down, and mentally rehearsed the motion of planting a bullet in each of the outlaws. Then he swung his gun towards Keating. His finger tightened on the trigger.

A shadow flickered beside his right

elbow. He glanced at it, thinking it was a high bird, but its outline was too crisp. And it was growing.

Lincoln glanced up to see a man slipping over the top of the boulder to his right, but the moment he saw Lincoln move, he leapt down on him. Lincoln had but a moment to react and so before he could even turn his gun on the man, he had landed on his back.

The blow knocked the air from his chest, as down below the noise made the three outlaws swing round to face them.

He braced himself and tried to buck the man off his back. The first attempt didn't move him so he jerked his elbow into the man's ribs, hearing him grunt in pain, then tried again. This time they both rolled over to land on their sides.

While holding him to his chest the man clawed at Lincoln's face, so Lincoln squirmed, trying to free himself. He dragged his left arm free, then aimed to tear away his gun hand, but before he could free it, a second man jumped down from the other boulder.

He landed lightly then kicked out, the toe of his boot thudding into Lincoln's chin and sending both him and his assailant rolling. When he came to a halt Lincoln lay stunned against the other man.

He flexed his fingers, finding that his gun had come free. Then he was dragged to his feet, stood upright, and grounded with a swinging blow to the jaw.

Unable to stop his motion, Lincoln rolled down the slope to come to rest at Lawrence Shannon's feet. He lay, catching his breath and willing his senses to return, but before they had, Lawrence tipped him over with a boot.

'Now what do we have here?' Lawrence gloated, looking down at him. 'It looks like we have a lawman. You aiming to arrest us?'

Keating and Billy chortled at Lawrence's wit while the other two men paced down to stand around him.

Lincoln looked up at the circle of

watchers. He didn't recognize the two men who had unexpectedly appeared and overwhelmed him, although he couldn't help but notice they wore cassocks.

He put aside that observation and thought of survival. He judged that his only hope lay with Richmond, and he presumed he hadn't shot at the outlaws yet for fear of hitting him.

So he levered himself to a sitting position and flexed his shoulders, deciding that when he got the chance he'd rush the nearest man and then while he subdued him, Richmond could launch an assault on the others.

'You're in deep trouble,' Lincoln said. His comment received another burst of confident laughter along with a few oaths. 'Surrender now while you still can.'

His bravado bought him a few more moments to regain his strength as the outlaws looked at each other and enjoyed their apparent success.

'How you planning to make us do

that, lawman?' Keating asked.

'I'm not the only one who's come for you. I've got men all around these rocks watching you and waiting for my signal.'

Despite it being unlikely that anyone else was here, the outlaws glanced around and, taking that as his only chance to fight back, Lincoln jumped to his feet and threw himself at the nearest man, Billy.

He wrapped his arms around his chest and carried him backwards for several paces, but Billy stuck in a heel and avoided being tipped over.

Then as the others swirled round to face them, the two men tussled. They rocked one way then the other, but neither man made headway as Lincoln ensured he kept Billy held tightly to avoid the others shooting him.

He willed Richmond to act, but even though the other four men were standing in clear space and providing easy targets, he didn't act.

Then Billy managed to loop a foot

around Lincoln's knee and tugged, making him stumble to the side. With a great roar of triumph Billy pushed him away.

Lincoln's grip came loose and he hit the ground on his side then rolled to come to rest on his back, looking up at the outlaws.

They formed a line, their guns drawn and aimed down at him. Lawrence smirked as he sighted Lincoln's chest.

Lincoln raised his chin while still hoping that Richmond's intervention would come before it was too late.

Then from the corner of his eye he saw movement behind the outlaws as Richmond stepped into view in the gap between the boulders, his gun drawn and raised. He avoided looking at him and fixed Lawrence with his gaze.

'Kill me,' he said, talking merely to give Richmond enough time to act, 'and every lawman in the state will hunt you down and kill you.'

'Dead men don't get hunted, but whether you live or die isn't up to us.'

Behind them Richmond continued to advance, and he wasn't walking with stealth.

The outlaws were sure to hear him approach and so Lincoln wasn't surprised when Lawrence flinched then turned to look at Richmond. He registered surprise only with a raised eyebrow.

'Lawrence Shannon,' Richmond said, pacing closer, 'Billy Maxwell and Keating Dobbs all in one place, along with two others I haven't seen before. So what do we do now?'

'That's up to you,' Lawrence said.

Richmond nodded then looked around, taking in the line of outlaws and Lincoln. Just before he spoke, Lincoln saw the slight narrowing of his eyes and his smirk.

Lincoln's guts turned to ice as he realized what was happening here and why Richmond had been acting strangely.

He hadn't become incompetent.

It was all an act.

'We can't risk alerting the mission with even a single gunshot,' Richmond said. He pointed at the two men who had jumped Lincoln. 'So take him away and kill him quietly.'

8

'Any luck?' Cameron asked when Jack joined him after exploring his side of the mission.

Jack shook his head. 'Nobody saw Gaston steal the ring, or leave the mission, or even saw him do anything. And the only clue I've found doesn't help us either.'

He led Cameron to the stable where a side wall that had been whole yesterday had been knocked through.

'What am I looking at?' Cameron asked, peering through the hole and merely seeing the nearest stall.

'Apparently, last night someone took the wall apart. Also a length of rope is missing.'

'But that doesn't explain where he went.'

Jack shrugged. 'Perhaps he went over the mission wall and he needed a pile of bricks to stand on — '

Cameron pointed into the stable. 'Instead of just taking his horse and getting away.'

'Which means he's not gone far, and we've still got hope.'

They stood silently for a while with neither man feeling hopeful, until Cameron saw Father Raphael coming out of the chapel.

With no ideas coming to them, they headed off to question him about the mission's layout, hoping there might be somewhere where they hadn't searched, but as it turned out, Raphael was just as interested in questioning them.

'Father Bartholomew says I should help you,' he said, his tone more flustered than the calm and benevolent attitude he'd shown last night. 'He has impressed upon me the urgency of the situation, and he has asked me to convey that to you.'

Cameron rubbed a sore rib ruefully. 'We were impressed with the urgency last night, but that hasn't helped us. We still have no idea where Gaston's gone.'

'If anywhere,' Jack said.

'A thorough search was completed last night by men who are more familiar with the mission than you are. So he must have left.' Raphael frowned. 'But perhaps we should postpone discussing this matter until we have begun our search outside the mission.'

Cameron nodded and gestured for Raphael to take the lead. When they'd mounted up and ridden through the mission gateway, he asked the obvious question.

'Where should we search?'

'I had hoped you would have an idea where to look,' Raphael said. 'I'm afraid I don't understand men like Gaston Prix. I am used to spending time with men of a more spiritual inclination, such as Father Bartholomew.'

Cameron and Jack glanced at each other, sharing their thoughts on the matter with raised eyebrows. Then Cameron looked around for a likely place that Gaston could have reached on foot without being seen.

An outcrop of rocks faced the gateway a mile away, but he judged that as being too obvious a place to go for someone as sneaky as Gaston was.

In the other direction, a half-mile away, a creek emerged from the ground then moved on to twist past the mission. With no better idea in mind, Cameron pointed and nudged his horse on towards the water.

They had halved the distance when he broached the uncomfortable subject.

'Do you enjoy being in Father Bartholomew's care?' he asked Raphael.

'Enjoyment is not a part of the life I have chosen,' Raphael said.

Cameron accepted that Raphael was as he appeared, a devout man who saw the best in everyone, but he judged that his guarded comment hinted that he understood what was on Cameron's mind.

'But is Bartholomew, shall we say, perhaps too devoted to ensuring people don't enjoy life?'

Raphael gave a brief laugh. 'Father Bartholomew is a driven man of vision. He has made it his singular aim to restore the mission to its former status. I share that vision.'

Cameron conceded that comment with a nod, but Jack spoke up.

'Do Father Steven and Father Joshua share that vision?' he asked.

They had learnt the names of the fist-wielding padres after their beating last night, and even if Raphael didn't know of that event, he winced. When he spoke his voice was low and troubled.

'I fail to see why you are questioning our actions when it is clearly Gaston who has erred.'

'Because,' Cameron said, 'to steal the ring when the statue was supposed to be guarded and then to disappear so effectively, Gaston probably had help.'

'When we give our lives to the Lord's work, our past lives cease to exist.' Raphael bunched his jaw, suggesting he was battling with himself as to whether to mention something. 'But those two brothers, Steven and Joshua, joined the mission this month. Bartholomew uses them for disciplinary matters as they did have something of a . . . a colourful background.'

While Jack grunted and rubbed his ribs, clearly recalling the beating he'd received last night, Cameron sighed, now reckoning they were making progress.

'Are they still in the mission?'

'They left after matins.' Raphael looked along the creek to the point where the water came spurting out from its underground passage. When he spoke his tone sounded guilty, as if he were betraying a confidence. 'They often go there for silent contemplation.'

'Then maybe we should join them in that silent contemplation.'

Raphael's wince showed he'd caught Cameron's sarcasm, but he nodded with good grace and so they headed on along a route parallel to the creek.

As the roaring water emerged it created a mist through which a rainbow shone, but despite the noise, an occasional raised voice came to them.

'An argument?' Jack said. 'Surely that's not right for padres engaged in silent contemplation.'

Raphael said nothing although Cameron smiled as all three men hurried their horses on.

Through the mist, the two padres became visible along with a third man. They were moving around, although as they were 200 yards away and had their backs to them, it was unclear what they were doing.

The group didn't notice them approaching and Cameron was content for that to continue as he hoped the third man was Gaston, but closer to he saw that he was too large to be their quarry. And he was fighting with the padres.

'This is most unseemly,' Raphael said.

They speeded up, hurrying on to reach them.

As they drew up, the padres saw that they had company and spun round to face them, letting Cameron see that they hadn't exactly been fighting.

The third man was being held up and they had been taking it in turns to pummel him. The man now stood bent over, only Joshua's arm around his waist keeping him upright.

'Are you administering to the infirm, then?' Cameron said, 'or are you making him infirm?'

Steven and Joshua stood together to consider them, their expressions displaying a mixture of the contempt they'd shown last night along with concern that Raphael was here.

'We,' Steven murmured, 'don't have to explain nothing to you.'

'You don't,' Raphael said, his tone becoming strident and authoritative for the first time. 'But you will explain it to me.'

The two men glanced at each other, silently debating what they should do. Then Steven spread his hands and offered a guarded smile.

'We were searching for the missing

ring when we saw this man acting suspiciously. We were trying to find out what he knew.'

'By beating him senseless?'

'Father Bartholomew has impressed upon us the urgency of the situation.'

At the mention of Bartholomew, Raphael sighed and his voice became less stern.

'I commend you for your diligence, but this is not the right way. We will take him back to the mission and care for him.'

Steven glanced at the man, seeing that he was unconscious.

'As you wish,' he said.

It was only when Joshua had let the man fall to the ground that Cameron recognized him. He was the lawman who had saved them from a showdown with Billy Maxwell, Marshal Lincoln Hawk.

★   ★   ★

Lincoln opened his eyes, already tensing himself in anticipation of the next blow, but he found to his surprise that he was no longer beside the creek.

He looked around and saw that he was lying on his back on the floor within a large building, with a vaulted ceiling high above him.

With a flinch he realized that he was in the chapel within the mission.

How he had come to be here he didn't know. He moved to get up, then regretted it when a dull pain tore through his chest.

A grunt escaped his lips and this drew attention to him. The man who came over wore a cassock of the same kind as Steven and Joshua had worn.

He moved to get away from him, again finding that he failed to move far before the pain in his chest made him wish he hadn't tried.

'Stay,' the man said with a kindly voice.

'Who are you?' Lincoln croaked through swollen lips.

'I'm Father Raphael. I found you when two of our brethren were being somewhat overzealous in their pursuit of a solution to our little problem.'

Lincoln glared up at Raphael, unable to work out if he was a fool or if he was covering up for the men who'd planned to kill him, but he decided he was too weak to work it out. He settled down, looking up at the high ceiling.

'How bad?'

'You have extensive bruising, but nothing is broken. We have bathed and cleaned your wounds. Later we will bind your chest and then you will feel more comfortable. For now all you can do is rest.'

Lincoln nodded. He looked aloft and listened to Raphael pace away then talk to two men in low tones, advising them on how to treat his injuries. As they talked, a louder voice interrupted.

'Who is he?' the new man demanded.

'He's a lawman, Father Bartholomew.'

'Does he know where Gaston Prix went?'

'I don't believe he was looking for him, but he's not in a fit state to confirm that.'

'I need answers. He has an hour.' Two sets of receding footfalls sounded and when Bartholomew spoke again his voice was barely discernible. 'But you have no excuses.'

Raphael murmured an answer. Lincoln couldn't hear the words, but his uncertain tone suggested he was playing for time. While he struggled to overhear their conversation, two other men approached him.

Lincoln craned his neck to see them come to a halt standing over him. Both men were familiar.

'I hope you're fine,' one man said.

'I will be,' Lincoln said, searching the man's face as he attempted to place where he'd seen him before.

'We helped you.' The man looked at Raphael and Bartholomew. 'So we'd welcome you helping us by telling Bartholomew what we did.'

'I'll be sure to tell him.' Lincoln winced on realizing where he'd seen these men before. They had been playing poker in Pandora with Billy

Maxwell. Back then he'd assumed they were innocent, but now they were in a mission that Billy was preparing to attack, something so unlikely it couldn't be a coincidence. 'I'll tell him everything he needs to know to stop you carrying out the raid.'

'You've got us wrong,' Cameron said, backing away a pace and raising his hands. 'We don't know nothing about no raid.'

Lincoln snorted then raised his head to look towards the door.

'Father Bartholomew,' he shouted. 'There's something you need to know about these men.'

9

'Father Bartholomew won't believe him,' Jack said.

'I hope not,' Cameron said. He pointed to the chapel where Bartholomew was emerging after his discussion with the marshal. 'But I guess we'll find out soon enough.'

They waited apprehensively until he joined them.

'I had thought you were in league with Gaston Prix,' Bartholomew said. 'Instead it appears you are in league with outlaws who are planning to raid the mission.'

Cameron gulped. 'Marshal Hawk is hurt and he's not thinking straight. We don't know nothing about no outlaws, or a raid, or even about Gaston's plans. I mean, if we were planning to raid the mission, would we have rescued him?'

Bartholomew considered this with his jaw set firm, his failure to snap back a response suggesting he thought the answer to be a reasonable one.

'It's difficult to see why you'd do that, but then again if you're working with the devious Gaston, I dread to think what kind of scheme you have in mind. But I know one way you can convince me.'

'We'll take it.'

Bartholomew grinned with a wide smirk that suggested they would regret that acceptance, then wrapped an arm around each man's shoulders and shepherded them towards a gap in the mission wall. He pointed at the outcrop of rocks a mile away.

'See those rocks?' he asked.

'Yes,' Cameron said, cautiously. 'We'd considered looking for Gaston there.'

'That was an excellent plan because according to Marshal Hawk, three outlaws and a bounty hunter are holed up there waiting to raid the mission. I want you to find out if he's right.'

Cameron winced. 'If they're there, they'll kill us.'

'I know, but at least you'll prove your innocence while revealing the truth.' Bartholomew released his arms then shoved them forward.

They stopped and looked at Bartholomew, but he returned a grim glare and behind him Joshua and Steven edged into the chapel doorway to watch them. So without enthusiasm Cameron and Jack trooped to their horses.

Five minutes later they were again plodding out through the main gateway, this time with even less enthusiasm than the previous time.

As they rode towards the outcrop, they said nothing while pensively running their gazes along the top of the rocks, looking out for any sign of movement, but they saw nothing.

'Where do we search first?' Jack asked when they reached the outcrop.

'We need to stay at ground level.' Cameron patted his horse with a gesture that said that getting away quickly was his main priority.

Jack grunted that he understood and so they worked their way around the base. They looked at every boulder they passed, but they saw nothing untoward.

The mission was slipping out of view, letting them see the other side of the outcrop, when Jack stopped and voiced what was on Cameron's mind.

'We can't see much,' he said. 'We'll have to explore on foot.'

Cameron gave a reluctant nod and so they jumped down from their horses and hurried, bent over, to the nearest boulder.

When they reached it they stood with their backs to the rock enjoying the feeling of being relatively safe as they were hidden from the bulk of the outcrop. Then they hurried to the next boulder where they again stopped.

Moving in this cautious manner they gradually gained height, but although they could see the surrounding plains there were many boulders behind which someone could hide, so the terrain closer to wasn't so visible.

Cameron was about to voice the unwelcome thought that they should split up so they could cover more ground when he heard a horse neigh.

Jack tensed and they both looked down at their horses, but they were standing quietly. Without conferring they both picked out the spot from where the sound had come, a point to their right. Then they set off.

A second sound came, of grit moving over grit.

Then the cold steel of a gun barrel dug into the back of Cameron's neck.

'What you doing here?' a voice said behind him.

'You're not Gaston Prix,' Cameron said, offering the only excuse for them being here that he could think of.

'No, I'm Lawrence Shannon. Who's Gaston?'

'He's just someone we were looking for and we thought he'd be here. We didn't mean to cause you no trouble. We'll go.'

Cameron moved to go, but Lawrence clapped a hand on his shoulder, halting him.

'It doesn't work like that. You came from the mission.'

Lawrence nudged Cameron forward then gestured for Jack to join him in walking along on a route around the nearest boulder.

As they walked, Cameron looked over his shoulder at their captor and offered a smile.

'We don't have to go back there if you don't want us to.'

'I'm not taking the risk of alerting them, so you're staying here.'

Cameron stopped and glanced at Jack, who conveyed that he'd understood what was on his mind with a slight narrowing of the eyes.

'In that case . . . ' Cameron jerked himself to the side to get away from Lawrence and, in a coordinated move, Jack turned on his heel and threw himself at their captor. He grabbed his gun and thrust it high, then pushed him sideways into the boulder.

Lawrence grunted as his shoulder and gun arm collided with the rock.

Jack slammed him against the rock a second time as he concentrated on disarming him. On his third shove Lawrence's gun came free, by which time Cameron had joined the fray. He grabbed Lawrence's shoulder and together they bundled him to the ground.

Lawrence fell heavily and lay in a sprawled heap before he slid away from them. With frantic arm-waving and kicking he fought for purchase, but he was unable to still his progress and he speeded up then tumbled down the slope.

Cameron and Jack didn't wait to see if he managed to stop his progress and they ran around the outcrop.

They'd covered forty yards and had rounded two large boulders when Cameron saw movement from the corner of his eye. He turned to see Billy Maxwell leaping out at them.

Again they took advantage of the outlaw's desire to capture them quietly.

Cameron grappled with Billy while Jack ducked down and grabbed him around the waist.

They combined to bundle him to the ground, whereupon a firm kick from Jack's boot sent him rolling away down the slope. Then they moved on.

'That's two down,' Jack said, happily, 'two to go.'

'Yeah,' Cameron said. He pointed at a route that would take them around the back of the outcrop and get them back to ground level. 'But I reckon we should go for our horses before our luck runs out.'

Jack grunted that he agreed, but they'd managed only another twenty paces when both men skidded to a halt, the sight ahead shocking them.

On the other side of the outcrop were riders, and not just the two remaining men they'd been told about. Cameron counted at least twenty men while glimpsing others between outlying boulders, and they were all approaching the outcrop, taking a route that kept them out of view from the mission.

Then several of those men looked at them.

Cameron and Jack didn't wait to see what they did next. They turned on their heels and hurtled down the slope away from the men.

As they bounded from rock to rock in their aim of getting to their horses as quickly as possible they saw Lawrence and Billy closing in from the side, aiming to cut them off. Both men were hobbling after tumbling down to ground level but they compensated for their slow paces with their determined postures.

When Cameron and Jack reached the ground they were thirty yards from their horses; the two approaching men were the same distance away. As they set off Cameron looked over his shoulder.

Dozens of riders were swarming around the outcrop and every one of them had a gun levelled on them.

'We raid now,' Lawrence shouted, gesturing to them. 'So just kill 'em!'

10

'Does that feel better?' Father Raphael asked, standing back to appraise his work.

Lincoln felt his bandaged ribs, finding that the bulky strapping limited his movement but that it also reduced the discomfort.

He'd avoided getting cracked ribs and the rest of his torso was merely badly bruised, so he'd come out of his ordeal in better condition than he'd had any right to expect.

'It does,' Lincoln said as Raphael helped him into his waistcoat and then jacket.

Raphael gave a short bow then turned away. Lincoln moved to follow him, but Raphael turned back and raised a hand.

'Stay here,' he said. 'Only rest will complete your recovery.'

'I can't afford to rest. Raiders are out there and two of your padres are helping them.' Lincoln walked to the door of the chapel to look out, taking in the extent of the mission grounds. 'We perhaps have only minutes to organize a defence.'

Raphael joined him at the door. 'Defence is not an option. No matter how aggrieved you feel about Steven and Joshua's actions, we are men of God and we do not raise arms against our fellow man.'

'Then if you haven't got the guts to defend the mission, is there anyone here who will?'

Raphael let the insult pass without changing his benign expression.

'The people in the settlement are old or infirm and need protecting, not to join in any fighting.'

Lincoln considered the mission walls, noting the lack of a gate and the numerous sections of wall that had fallen away, thereby providing the raiders with ready access.

'Then unless I can find a way to defend this place they and everyone else here will die.' Lincoln waited until Raphael began to shake his head, then continued. 'Take me to Father Bartholomew.'

During his time with Bartholomew, he'd decided he was more realistic in outlook than Raphael was. When Raphael acquiesced and led him to his boss, he found this to be the case, even if he also refused to take up arms.

'I've sent Cameron and Jack to find out if you're right,' Bartholomew said. 'If it turns out that you are, Francisco Quintos will help us.'

'As I am right, take me to him now.'

'I never disturb him during the day. And we had a problem last night. Until I can resolve that, I would prefer not to — '

Bartholomew screeched as Lincoln grabbed the collar of his cassock and dragged him up close. The action made his ribs protest, but the pain added extra commitment to his demand.

'You don't appreciate the trouble you're in. Cameron and Jack are helping the outlaws as are your padres Steven and Joshua. That's eight men set on raiding an indefensible mission and all you have is me and a group of yellow-bellies who won't raise a finger to save themselves. So if Francisco can do something more useful than pray, I need to see him. And now!'

Lincoln gripped his fist more tightly, making Bartholomew wince. Through his closed throat he bleated out a few words.

'I understand your need.'

Lincoln held on for a moment longer then opened his hand and let Bartholomew stand. Then he bade him to lead on.

Bartholomew glared at him. Then he took an inordinate amount of time to straighten his cassock and prepare to take him to see Francisco, providing a show of himself as still being in charge.

In a slow manner that was presumably designed to annoy Lincoln even more, he paced through the chapel.

Lincoln filed in behind him and said nothing, presuming that any complaint would only delay further his meeting with Francisco.

Bartholomew led him to a door behind a statue and into an enclosed courtyard beyond. On the opposite side there was another door that led into a one-storey building at which he knocked and waited for a summons.

Two guards ushered them into what turned out to be an ornately decorated room, presumably Francisco's living quarters.

A tall man was sitting at a table. He looked up, his jaw set firm.

'Why are you disturbing us?' he asked.

'I apologize,' Bartholomew said, 'to you and to José, but the marshal gave me no choice.'

Francisco considered Lincoln, taking in his bruised and battered face along with the star.

'You've seen some trouble,' he said in

a softer tone than before.

Lincoln glanced around the room, noting the old man, presumably José, sitting on a chair by the window, looking up at the chapel. He took no apparent interest in their arrival as he murmured to himself while rocking back and forth.

'Not as much as you will,' Lincoln said. 'Three ruthless outlaws and a renegade bounty hunter are close by. They've got it into their heads that you have gold hidden away in the mission. The bounty hunter has given the outlaws the alibi that they are in fact dead. That means they won't let anybody live to disprove it.'

Francisco dismissed this matter with a shrug. 'I employ two guards to look after my family and the mission. They will ensure the raiders fail.'

Lincoln glanced at the guards at the door, both of whom were eyeing him with suspicion despite knowing his status. Lincoln judged that as a sign that they were dutiful and capable.

'The problem's not just the raiders. They have help from two padres and two pilgrims who arrived last night.'

Bartholomew coughed as Lincoln mentioned the subject of his own brethren having ulterior motives.

'You shouldn't burden Francisco with that matter,' he said. 'He has already confirmed he has sufficient resources to cope.'

Francisco nodded then returned to considering the paperwork on his desk with the air of a man who had dismissed the matter from his mind.

'There's one more thing I need to know,' Lincoln said. He waited until Francisco looked up and registered mild interest with a raised eyebrow. 'The gold, is it here?'

Francisco snorted a laugh, as if a private joke amused him. Bartholomew edged from side to side in an animated manner as if this question amused him too.

'Have you met my father?' Francisco asked. Francisco gestured to José, drawing Lincoln's attention to the fact he hadn't changed his posture since he'd arrived.

'No, but I gather he's not well.'

Francisco got up from the table and went over to José. He laid a hand on his shoulder, again garnering no reaction, then faced Lincoln. When he spoke he adopted a resigned lecturing tone, as if this was something he'd said many times before.

'Ten years ago bandits destroyed his mind trying to make him talk, but no matter what they did to him, they didn't learn the truth.' Francisco gave José a firm pat on the shoulder then coughed to cover a catch in his throat. He returned to the table before he spoke again. 'So do you think that if their knives and their fires couldn't drag an answer from his lips, then you can get me to answer with a simple request?'

Lincoln glanced at José, who continued to look up at the chapel.

'I understand, but will you ever

reveal the truth?'

'Only after the bell sounds once more.' He pointed through the window at the bell tower, the top of which was out of view, presumably that being what José was looking at. 'My father used to toll it every sundown. When he dies I'll rebuild the steps and sound the bell again, but I won't talk about the gold until then.'

Lincoln lowered his voice. 'If things don't go well today, you may have to show the same fortitude as your father did.'

Francisco acknowledged this fact with a nod.

Then Lincoln and Bartholomew returned to the chapel where they were greeted by the sight of Father Raphael walking down the aisle and pointing through the main door.

'The raiders are coming,' he said simply.

'How long do we have?' Bartholomew asked, but Raphael didn't get a chance to answer as Lincoln barged past them and hurried off through the chapel.

The two padres followed at a more sedate pace. When they joined Lincoln, Bartholomew wasted no time in complaining.

'You will not treat me in such a disrespectful manner,' he proclaimed. 'As Francisco said, we can cope with anything these men do.'

'I don't reckon so,' Lincoln said from the doorway then moved aside to let them see what had disturbed him.

The three men stood in awed silence as they took in the sight beyond the mission walls. Cameron and Jack were galloping towards them side by side, while 500 yards behind them a solid line of men were riding on at a confident slow pace.

Lincoln counted thirty men and although they were too far away for him to discern who most of them were, he recognized the build of the middle group of four men: Lawrence Shannon's trio along with Richmond Cafferty.

'We cannot assume they mean to

attack us,' Raphael said. 'They may need our help. So we will welcome them as we would any traveller.'

Raphael moved away, his hands slipping into the sleeves of his cassock, his face already set in his pleasant greeting smile, but Bartholomew slapped a hand on his shoulder and halted him.

'In this case,' he said, 'it might be better to prepare for the worst.'

'Agreed,' Lincoln said. 'Raphael, get everyone together in the chapel. Bartholomew, alert Francisco and get those guards.'

'You will not order me,' Bartholomew snapped. He glared at Lincoln, but when Lincoln didn't retort, he turned to leave. 'But I will go to Francisco because I deem it the right thing to do.'

Then with a swirl of his cassock he moved away into the chapel.

Lincoln watched him to confirm he was carrying out his orders, even if Bartholomew chose to see them as his own, then followed on behind Raphael, who was calling out for everyone to join him.

Lincoln stopped at the gateway to await the twosome who he suspected were aiding Richmond Cafferty. Although when Cameron and Jack rode into the mission, they didn't appear as if they were helping him. Both men were galloping hard while glancing nervously over their shoulders at the advancing men.

It was possible that they were only appearing as if they were running from trouble, but on the other hand the raiders had such superior numbers they didn't need to employ subterfuge.

When the two men jumped down from their horses, shouting out about the trouble behind, Lincoln decided he'd give them the benefit of the doubt.

'So,' he said, feigning a jovial mood, 'at least you proved the raiders were at the outcrop.'

'They were, and we're doomed,' Cameron said, his voice high-pitched and scared as he pointed through the gateway.

'And you have to believe we're not helping them,' Jack said while staring aghast at the closing mass of guntoting raiders.

'I do believe you,' Lincoln said, receiving sighs of relief. He saw that Raphael and two other padres were returning through the gateway with the people from the settlement, but the men who had beaten him weren't amongst them. 'And trust me when I say we can prevail. But first we have to eliminate anyone here who we don't trust.'

'Steven and Joshua?' Cameron asked.

Lincoln patted his back. 'Exactly. Can you find them and make sure they cause us no further problems?'

Cameron gave a brief nod along with a smile that said he was thankful Lincoln had given them a task that stopped them having to dwell on the seemingly insurmountable problems ahead. With Jack, he hurried away, leaving Lincoln to consider how he'd deal with the rest.

He watched the riders close on the walls.

The only hope he could see was to dispose of the leading group then hope that the rest would lack the resolve to fight on. This hope receded when the four riders in the centre drew back, letting the others merge in to re-form the line.

They maintained this formation until they were a hundred yards from the gateway, where they split up. Half their number headed towards a crumbling stretch of wall to the left of the gateway while the other half headed towards a wide breach in the walls before the chapel.

Three of the leaders halted to watch their progress while Lawrence Shannon hurried on through the gap the others had created.

Raphael was still shepherding people towards the chapel but Lawrence was confident enough not to pay them any attention. This made Lincoln realize he did have one advantage.

Lawrence wouldn't expect him to be alive. So Lincoln backed away out of sight then hurried to the chapel.

Inside, Bartholomew had returned with the guards. Francisco had also come, but not his father, and he stood back, letting Lincoln command the guards.

Lincoln ordered them to take up positions flanking the door and to watch out for Bartholomew when he spoke to Lawrence.

As expected, Bartholomew bristled at being given such a direct order.

'You will not command me,' he said. 'You will inform me of the situation and I will decide what everyone should do.'

Lincoln set his hands on his hips. 'A whole heap of outlaws will arrive in one minute hell-bent on mayhem. What else do you need to know?'

Bartholomew firmed his jaw. 'Where are Cameron and Jack?'

'I've tasked them with finding your

renegade padres, Steven and Joshua, before they can join forces with the outlaws and make the situation even worse.'

Bartholomew's face reddened, this response appearing to concern him more than their predicament.

'They are not renegades, and I will prove it.'

With that pronouncement he set off, presumably to search for them, leaving Lincoln with no choice but to ask Raphael to speak with Lawrence. The padre took the order with a nod then followed Bartholomew through the door.

As Raphael veered away to the gateway, Lincoln turned his attention to the people in the chapel.

He saw that, as promised, none of the people Raphael had brought from the settlement would be able to help them. They were unarmed and they were all so old they walked with difficulty. Most were already resting on the pews after their short journey.

Then from beside the door, he watched how Raphael fared.

'You are all welcome,' Raphael called out to Lawrence when he came through the gateway. 'Direct your men to come inside and we will provide whatever food and shelter we can.'

Lawrence snorted as he drew up his horse. 'We want only one thing. Fetch José Quintos.'

'I'm afraid he is indisposed and his son Francisco is busy.'

Lawrence glanced over his shoulder at the line of advancing men. 'He won't be busy for this. Tell him I've come for the gold. Either he hands it over or I'll kill everyone in the mission, ending with his loco father and then him.'

Raphael spread his hands. 'You're mistaken. There's no gold here. All we have to offer is our hospitality.'

Lawrence leaned forward in the saddle. 'Then you will be the first to die.'

Raphael backed away for an voluntary pace then raised a hand.

'Wait here. I will see if — ' He coughed as Lawrence moved his hand towards his holster. Then he turned on his heel and, with the most haste Lincoln had seen him use, he ran back to the chapel.

'It's as I said, then?' Lincoln said when Raphael joined him and Francisco.

'He is most determined,' Raphael said. 'He says we will all die, unless you give him the gold.'

Francisco nodded, the demand not appearing to surprise him.

'The mission is lost, but not the chapel,' he said. 'Bar the door. Then we fight to the last.'

11

Cameron and Jack hurried to the stable, this being the last building they had left to search for the two renegade padres.

From here they couldn't see what was happening in front of the chapel, but Cameron could hear a commotion going on.

'That doesn't sound good,' he said.

'No,' Jack said, offering a smile. 'Although at least the raiders have taken Bartholomew's mind off finding Gaston by sundown.'

Cameron snorted a laugh at Jack's grim humour.

Then they peered into the stable through the side door and took in the rows of mainly empty stalls, but over in the final stall their quarries were standing. They were jerking back and forth, with their concentration being on something on the ground.

Cameron darted back. Then in hushed tones he debated their course of action with Jack.

The result was that they walked inside, crouched over, then made for the nearest stall. Then they worked their way along from stall to stall, all the time getting closer to their targets.

The quadrangle came into view through the doorway, letting them see that the raiders were filing in through the gateway. Cameron and Jack put that worrying sight from their minds as they hurried on past the remaining stalls.

They went past five stalls without either of their targets looking up, but then Jack tripped over a discarded pitchfork and went all his length with a thud.

He managed to keep his wits about him and rolled to the side into a stall. Cameron joined him, but when he hunkered down and peered out between two of the slats that fenced in the stalls, he saw that the padres were looking their way.

The two men headed towards them while peering around. Luckily they weren't sure where the noise had come from and so they walked into the stall beside the one in which Cameron and Jack were hiding.

Steven's gaze darted into the corners of the stall. In normal light he would be able to see their outlines easily but, with the sun being high and blasting down dazzling light through the roofless stable, he looked in their direction without registering their presence.

Then he glanced at Joshua and jerked his head to the side, suggesting they return to the end stall. Cameron watched them to ensure they were leaving then glanced at Jack and smiled, but Jack was looking up at him from the ground with his face set in a shocked expression.

Jack pointed, and so Cameron joined him in lying on the ground to see what had concerned him.

At ground level he could see along

the length of the stalls. In the end stall the body of Father Bartholomew was lying, sprawled and beaten, confirming what the two padres had been doing when they'd been interrupted.

That sight was enough for Cameron. He jumped to his feet and slammed his gun on the top of the stall.

'Raise those hands,' he demanded.

Steven stomped to a halt and did as he'd been told. Joshua turned but didn't raise his hands, even when Jack joined Cameron in holding a gun on them. Steven turned towards Joshua, appearing as if he'd tell him to follow the instruction and that made both Jack and Cameron turn to him.

Clearly that was the distraction they'd hoped to get.

Joshua thrust his right hand up his left sleeve, then yanked out a gun. Before he got to fire, Jack swung the gun back and blasted a slug that tore into Joshua's chest and sent him reeling backwards into the fence behind him.

As he crashed through it to land on

his back, Steven also thrust a hand up his sleeve. But before he could reach the weaponry hidden there Cameron caught him with a low shot to the guts that bent him double.

Steven stayed doubled over, staggered a pace, then straightened, his gun swinging up, his expression set grimly and showing his determination to fire. But he didn't get to before Cameron and Jack both fired at him.

Their twin shots slammed into Steven's chest and sent him staggering backwards through the broken fence to land beside Joshua.

Cameron and Jack waited with their guns drawn, seeing if they'd rise, but both men were still. Then they looked through the doorway.

'The raiders must have heard the gunfire,' Cameron said.

'Yeah,' Jack said, 'but hopefully they'll expect that when they're in the midst of a raid.'

Cameron murmured that he hoped so too, but that hope died when he saw several men move away from the chapel and head towards them. Before they could be seen, they hurried on to the end stall, but the sight that greeted them confirmed their worst fears.

Father Bartholomew was dead.

Neither man had reason to mourn him after the treatment he'd meted out to them, but at least his fate proved that he wasn't the same kind of man as Steven and Joshua had been.

It was too late to move the bodies and so Cameron pointed to the hole in the stable wall that had been made last night.

'Come on,' he said. 'If we move quickly, we might get lucky.'

Jack nodded and so they hurried to the hole. Voices could be heard outside as they reached it, so they slipped outside quickly, walking backwards to keep the doorway in view.

They'd taken only two paces when metal jabbed into Cameron's back a moment before he saw another man slap a gun up against Jack's neck.

'So it is Cameron and Jack, after all,' a familiar voice said from behind him. 'I thought it was you skulking over by the outcrop.'

Cameron glanced over his shoulder to see that he had been right about the man who had accosted them.

'Billy Maxwell,' he murmured.

'It is, and this sure is my lucky day.' Billy licked his lips. 'I get the gold and I get to make you two pay for beating me at poker.'

★ ★ ★

'We should be able to hold out behind this,' Francisco said approvingly as he slapped the closed chapel door.

Lincoln shook his head. 'What about Father Bartholomew and — '

'We will pray,' Raphael said, 'that they have found somewhere to hole up.'

Lincoln considered the closed door, but he judged he didn't have a choice.

'I doubt anywhere will be safe,' Francisco said, matching Lincoln's thoughts. He pointed at the scorch marks on the walls. 'When the last raid happened the door was even thicker, but they still burnt their way through.'

Francisco looked over his shoulder at the door that led to his house with an obvious gesture of concern for his father.

Then everyone reverted to silence as what was sure to become a tense waiting game started.

Surprisingly quickly, shuffling sounds came from behind the door as the raiders took up positions. Then Lawrence Shannon spoke up from the other side of the door with his demand.

'You people in there,' he shouted, his voice echoing in the otherwise quiet chapel. 'I only want the gold. Give it to me and you'll live. Defy me and you'll die.'

Lincoln stood back; still wishing to preserve the secret that he was alive, leaving Raphael to step up and respond.

'Many old people are in here,' he

called through the door, 'along with servants of God who hold no malice against you.'

Lawrence didn't respond for several seconds, giving the impression he was considering this statement seriously. When he spoke his voice was low.

'I want to believe you. So open the door and prove it.'

'We can't. This chapel is not a place for threats and violence.'

'It sure will be if you defy me. You have five minutes. If the door is still closed, the first two will die.' Lawrence spoke to someone outside in a low voice and received an answer. 'The condemned men are Cameron and Jack. They will not die easily. Their screams will chill your blood until sundown.'

Footfalls sounded as Lawrence stepped away from the door, leaving everyone inside to look at each other, waiting for someone to react. Raphael was that man.

'We can't let this happen,' he said, looking at Francisco. 'And I'm sure we all agree that this chapel is the most important consideration.'

Francisco looked at him. Neither man spoke, although each man's small facial movements suggested a silent debate was taking place. It concluded when Francisco turned to consider the padres and the old folk.

'Can you care for these people?' he asked.

'They have more hope under God's care than under that of the gun.'

'Then the place of worship will survive. I absolve you of all responsibility for what happens next.'

'And I absolve you.'

Francisco looked at Lincoln, his jaw set firmly as he appeared to consider telling him something. Then he turned on his heels and headed off down the chapel. His guards fell into line behind him as they made for the door back to his quarters.

Lincoln coughed, providing a nonverbal request for Francisco to explain himself. He waited for a response but

Francisco and the guards didn't break their stride. Lincoln didn't want to let the men outside know that he was here, so as he hurried after him he kept his voice low.

'Stop,' he said. 'You can't leave us.'

Francisco didn't look back, and followed the guards through the door behind the statue.

'He can,' Raphael said, blocking Lincoln's way. 'He's leaving the chapel to God's care. When he reaches his home, I will let the raiders in.'

Raphael moved towards the front door, but Lincoln grabbed his arm, swung him round, and marched him down the chapel after Francisco.

'Explain yourself,' he demanded.

Raphael dug in his heels and brought himself to a halt. Then, with a determined gesture, he tore his arm away from Lincoln, shrugged and set off walking.

'Francisco has promised that when he and his father have died, he will hand the mission back to the Church.'

Raphael slipped through the doorway to enter the small courtyard. 'So all that matters is this building and the good we, or those who come afterwards, can do here. Even the fate of Father Bartholomew is of less importance than that of the mission.'

'I'm not becoming a martyr.' Lincoln shoved him towards Francisco's house as the door closed. 'Speak to him. Keep him here.'

'He has made his decision.' An ominous thud sounded as the guards barred the door. 'I will trust in God to keep us safe in the chapel. Francisco will trust in the gun to keep the raiders away from his house.'

Lincoln pointed a firm finger at Raphael. 'You are not letting the raiders in.'

Raphael flashed a smile. 'While we have been talking, that demand has become irrelevant.'

Lincoln stared at him, wondering what he meant. Then with a wince he swung round to look into the chapel, and it was to see light flooding into the building.

At the opposite end one of the padres stood beside the open door, his hands outstretched as he welcomed the raiders outside to enter.

'You fools,' Lincoln murmured. 'You've condemned us all. The raiders' leaders are thought to be dead men. They won't let us live to disprove that.'

'If it is God's will that we die, we will,' Raphael said with a pious smile. Then he walked back into the chapel to welcome the raiders.

Lincoln swung round to place his back to the wall outside, keeping himself out of view as he listened to Lawrence and the others walk inside.

'You did the right thing,' Lawrence proclaimed from inside the chapel. 'Now where's Francisco?'

'He left the chapel,' Raphael said, 'through that door.'

Richmond joined Lawrence, and after a grunted exchange of views Lawrence agreed to investigate.

On his own, Lincoln was now too late and too outnumbered to drive away the raiders, the door beside him was flimsy, and on the other side of the enclosed courtyard the door to Francisco's quarters had been barred. There was no way out and no way to avoid being discovered in a matter of moments.

Desperately he looked around the courtyard, seeking cover.

Then his gaze rose to the chapel wall that towered above him. A smile tugged at his lips.

12

Billy Maxwell took a firm grip of Cameron's and Jack's arms then shoved them into the chapel.

'Just because the padre relented,' Billy said when he followed them in, 'you shouldn't go thinking that I've forgotten about you.'

Billy glared at them, his hand brushing a knife at his belt with obvious intent. Then he pushed them towards the padres and others who had gathered at the side of the chapel.

As up until a few moments ago when the door had surprisingly swung open they had been expecting to die, Cameron and Jack did their best to last out their luck by staying inconspicuous.

Richmond Cafferty and the other leaders stopped in the middle of the chapel to await Lawrence Shannon's verdict. After a few moments spent looking through the door, Lawrence returned.

'It's as Raphael said,' he reported. 'Francisco's taken refuge in his house.'

'Then he'll die in there,' Richmond said. He swung round to face Raphael. 'Unless you can persuade him to come out.'

'I have no control over him.' Raphael gestured around him. 'This chapel is the Lord's domain. The house and the gold, if it exists, is his.'

'Is that so?' Lawrence said.

Lawrence glared at Raphael, his piercing gaze suggesting that he would question him again later. Then he gathered the raiders around him in discussion.

They talked in harsh voices with much glancing around the chapel as if they expected deception from some quarter.

'We can take him,' Richmond said.

'We can,' Lawrence said, 'but fighting our way across twenty yards of open ground will be costly. Francisco will make us pay with blood for every step we take.'

'Then we need cover.' Richmond pointed at the pews. 'Rip up anything that can be moved and throw it through the door.'

Lawrence nodded then gestured to the raiders to carry out Richmond's orders. Only when they picked up the first pew and began to manoeuvre it towards the front of the chapel did Raphael complain.

'This is a chapel,' he said, walking towards Richmond and Lawrence. 'Please do not defile it.'

'Wood can be replaced,' Lawrence said with a significant glance at the smoke-damaged wall, 'so quit complaining or this time I will burn this place to the ground.'

Raphael rocked back and forth, looking as if he'd continue to push his luck, but then he turned on his heels and rejoined the others.

When the raiders reached the door they unceremoniously dumped the pew outside by pushing it upright then tipping it over. Then they returned for a second pew.

Cameron could see that before long they would create a barrier behind which they could launch an assault on Francisco's house, but even so, he judged that it would be a hard-fought battle.

Accordingly, he edged towards Jack and caught his eye then glanced at the three men who had been left guarding them. These men had clearly deemed their captives to be harmless, as they were paying less attention to them than they were to the preparations for the forthcoming battle.

With the leaders congregating beside the statue and those not engaged in creating a barrier lining up along one wall, Cameron reckoned these three men were the only ones they needed to worry about.

'Just give the word,' Jack whispered from the corner of his mouth, 'and we'll try something.'

'But can we run away and leave the others?' Cameron whispered.

'I reckon they'll be safer without us.' Jack considered. 'And besides, if we can get away, we can fetch help. That'll be more use than trying to take anyone with us or trying to take on thirty men.'

Cameron nodded then leaned back against the wall to watch their guards, waiting for the chance he hoped would come.

★   ★   ★

Lincoln hugged the wall, his boots scrambling for purchase until he located another foothold. Then he raised himself for another precarious foot.

He paused for breath and to give his bruised ribs a chance to stop throbbing. Yet again, he couldn't help but look down at the courtyard below.

The movement and his dizzying view of the ground, now far enough away to break bones if he slipped, made him sway, but it confirmed that after the crash of the pew in the courtyard, nobody had emerged.

So far he had been lucky and the few men who had dared to look into the courtyard hadn't looked upwards, but he didn't reckon that luck could hold out for long.

He pushed himself upwards towards the next foothold then moved his hands to a higher position. This movement sent him towards the corner of the tower.

He was now forty feet off the ground but still twenty feet from the windows that surrounded the area where the bell had once dangled.

He didn't want to risk being seen from the front of the chapel, but when a second pew went crashing to the ground below, he decided it wouldn't be long before men came into the courtyard.

So he moved towards the corner. He edged along the seam of stonework he was resting on, then peered around the side. With relief he saw that nobody was at the front of the chapel, as presumably everyone had gone inside.

From the corner of his eye he looked into the courtyard to see the two dropped pews lying in a cross formation.

A third pew was edging out towards them, the men pushing it remaining hidden in case of gunfire, but with the increasing level of cover available, the guards in the house stayed their fire.

Lincoln slipped a foot around the corner and found a foothold on the front of the chapel. Then, when he felt secure, he moved his right hand round to the front, found a solid grip, than manoeuvred himself around the corner.

This was the most dangerous action he'd tried to perform so far and for one terrible moment he teetered as his balance shifted, but then the bulk of his body slipped around to the front.

With his body plastered to the wall he caught his breath.

Then he looked up and picked out his route to the front window. He was relieved to see that on this side the prevailing wind had scoured out many crannies in which he could find purchase.

He reached up to the next handhold then placed a foot on the next ledge, but when he pressed down his foot broke through the stone and he lurched dangerously to the side.

He clung on, only his handhold ensuring he didn't tumble head first to the ground, as he watched the dislodged shards patter to the ground beside the chapel door.

Then he managed to find his original foothold and slowly he righted himself. All the time he looked down, waiting to act if someone emerged, but then he forced himself to look away, deciding that if anyone were to come out he stood no chance of defending himself in such an exposed position.

Speed in getting to the window above was his only option.

He sought out his next hold with greater care, gathering that the weather may have dug more holes but they were less stable ones. He saw a large gap at around knee level and so he raised his foot to it, then walked his fingers up the wall to the next hold and raised himself.

This time it held, as did the next hold as, with steady care, he closed on the window.

He again heard wood crash to the ground in the courtyard and the raiders must have become bolder as for the first time a volley of gunshots rang out from the house.

The raiders didn't return fire as they concentrated on building their barrier.

At the front of the chapel Lincoln reached up and felt a wide ledge. He glanced up to confirm it was the window then slapped both hands down on the ledge and drew himself up.

When he got his elbows planted on the ledge his weight crushed his bruised ribs but he still breathed a sigh of relief. Then he kicked up a leg and rolled over the ledge to land inside the tower.

The bell itself was lying on its side on the base of the small room, its weight being taken up on a small pile of bricks. He placed a hand on it to steady himself then moved to go round it, but he'd taken only a single pace when he flinched backwards in surprise.

He wasn't the only man here.

On the other side of the bell a man was crouched down with a gun aimed up at him.

'So you decided to hide up here too,' the man said, 'did you, Marshal Lincoln Hawk?'

'I took my only chance.' Lincoln considered the gun. 'But who's made the mistake of holding a gun on a lawman?'

'I'm the man everyone was looking for before those raiders distracted them.' The man smiled. 'I'm Gaston Prix.'

13

'Gaston Prix,' Lincoln said, eyeing the man in the tower. 'Father Raphael saved me when he was looking for you, but I never got to hear what your crime was.'

'I've committed no crime. I'm merely using an . . . an opportunity.'

Lincoln looked at the gun. 'A man who is only using an opportunity would be wise to holster that gun.'

Gaston kept the gun on him for a moment longer. Then with a shrug he lowered it.

'I was just protecting myself until I was sure who you were.'

'And as I need every armed man I can get, I'll choose to accept that.' Lincoln lowered himself to sit with his back against the wall, facing Gaston on the other side of the bell. 'So what is this opportunity?'

Gaston bit his lip, suggesting he was debating whether to answer, then glanced at the objects he'd set out around him, including a bundle of provisions, a ring and a long rope.

Then he nodded as if he'd made a decision and pointed at the bell.

'I guess you'll find out anyhow. Look in there.'

Lincoln did as requested. Tucked up inside the bell were numerous bags tied at the top and stacked in neat rows.

He reached in and hefted the nearest bag, feeling its weight and hearing the heavy clank of coins knocking together.

'José's stash of gold?' he said.

Gaston frowned then crawled over to the corner of the small room. Here the fire that had marred the front of the chapel had charred the walls and in the corner the floor had fallen away to leave an open space.

He pointed down through the hole with a finger to his lips then rejoined Lincoln and in a whisper replied.

'It is.'

Lincoln crawled over to the hole and looked down. He swayed, a moment of giddiness overcoming him when he saw that there was nothing beneath him other than the chapel floor sixty feet below.

Dotted around were the raiders with their captives having grouped together by a wall. At the front of the chapel three men were dragging another pew towards the door.

Nobody was looking up, but Lincoln decided that for now he wouldn't observe the happenings below and risk being seen, so he rejoined Gaston. 'How did you figure out the gold was up here?'

'I've been coming here for years and finally I pieced together the truth.' Gaston smiled proudly. 'José rang this bell every evening or when there was trouble, except he didn't ring it when the worst trouble this mission had ever seen happened. I wondered if perhaps that was because he didn't want to draw attention to the bell tower itself.'

'Perhaps,' Lincoln said nodding encouragingly.

'After the fire, Francisco didn't rebuild the steps despite his father's interest in the bell.' Gaston glanced at the bags within the bell. 'And I figured out why. José had stored the gold up here. When the fire burnt away the steps it let this tower become the one place nobody could search. So I gave everybody a distraction by stealing a ring. Then I planned to sit it out until I could sneak away with the gold.'

'I'm impressed.' Lincoln waited until Gaston smiled then firmed his expression to a stern glare. 'But that doesn't mean I'll let you steal it.'

Gaston rocked his head from side to side, seeming unperturbed by this threat.

'I can wait up here for longer than the raiders can, and for longer than you can if you want to help the captives.' Gaston licked his lips. 'And after you've been shot to hell and the raiders have done their worse, I'll sneak away with the gold.'

'That's a mighty fine plan.' Lincoln waited until Gaston relaxed then lunged out and grabbed his collar. He pulled him up tight to glare at him nose to nose. 'Except there's a problem. You're helping me, and if I get shot to hell, you will be too.'

Gaston gulped. 'I live by my wits. I'm no guntoter.'

'If you don't want me to tip you out the tower and dash those wits to the ground, you will help.' Lincoln heard a crash below as another pew fell into place. 'And besides in a location as good as this tower you don't need to be a guntoter.'

Lincoln dragged Gaston to his feet then pushed him towards the window overlooking the courtyard, but Gaston jerked back to remain out of view from the house.

Lincoln let him remain hidden for now as he looked down.

He saw foreshortened figures peering through the broken windows of Francisco's house. Then he craned his neck to look at the debris outside the door.

The raiders had done well in throwing the pews into positions that provided them with cover, and accordingly when the first two men crawled out of the door they weren't fired upon. They beckoned over their shoulders and two more men crawled out, following their path then lay down beside them.

After five minutes eight men had taken up positions, all presumably without being seen. None of them were the leaders, and so they waited for the signal to open fire.

Then the order must have come because as one they nudged up and peppered a prolonged volley of gunfire at the windows.

The raiders ducked down as the retaliatory gunfire exploded around them, kicking splinters from the tops of the pews, but failing to hole the wood. Then both groups set in to a routine of blasting at each other whenever they saw an opening.

Lincoln bided his time before making

his presence known, waiting until he could use the element of surprise to act in the most helpful manner.

After fifteen minutes of sporadic gunfire, Lincoln hadn't seen anyone from either group get wounded, but the attackers were making headway. Whenever there was a lull they kicked their covering piles of wood forward or spread them out, gradually getting themselves into better positions.

This meant the stalemate couldn't last for long and so Lincoln wasn't surprised when he heard a cry of pain come from the house.

This distracted one of the defenders and a moment later a deadly shot tore into that man and sent him staggering forward to lie sprawling out of the window with his arms dangling.

Heartened by their success the raiders in the flanking positions laid down a barrage of sustained gunfire while lead flew from the chapel doorway.

Then in the centre two men ran

doubled over for the doorway. They reached either side of it without mishap. Then in a coordinated move they acted.

One man reached in through a small grill in the door and fired indiscriminately. The other man shot at the lock, then put a shoulder to the door. The door was too well-barred for this to work, so he gestured to the chapel, requesting orders for their next actions.

Lincoln didn't wait to find out what they might be. He grabbed Gaston's shoulder, raised him into position, then pointed down at the courtyard.

'Fire,' he grunted, 'or you'll join them.'

Gaston gulped, but he provided a frantic nod, so Lincoln released him.

He didn't wait to see if he'd follow out his orders and took aim at the nearest of the men by the door. He fired, his first shot tearing into the man's chest and sending him reeling into the door.

The other man looked around,

the surprise in his eyes visible from the tower, but his gaze centred on the chapel door as he presumed the shot man had been caught in crossfire. Lincoln didn't let him wonder, as he dispatched him with a shot to the chest.

Then he turned his attention on the men hiding behind the pews, and he found that Gaston was already making headway.

He'd hit one man, leaving him lying over the pew before him. A second shot wounded the man beside him, making him jerk up in pain, whereupon the remaining guard in the house sent him tumbling on to his back.

With so much gunfire echoing in the confined space, none of the attackers had realized yet that gunfire was raining down on them from an unexpected direction.

Before they thought to look upwards, Lincoln turned his attention on the remaining raiders.

These men had gone to ground, not risking bobbing up to face the house. If he were to hit them, it would be clear to anyone looking on from the chapel that the gunfire couldn't have come from the house, but Lincoln reckoned he couldn't win through by being cautious.

He took aim at the furthest man and planted a bullet in his chest, then moved on to the others. With the men being further away it needed a dozen shots but, with Gaston's help, within a minute the eight raiders lay still.

Lincoln patted Gaston's back acknowledging his help, then hurried over to the hole in the floor.

The view looking down still made him giddy, but he was pleased to see that nobody was looking upwards nor was anyone near the door. Richmond and the other leaders were storming down the chapel, beckoning for the rest of the raiders to join them in discussion.

He considered opening fire, but there were too many of them and innocent people would suffer if he tried to decimate the raiders and failed. So he jerked back before anyone chanced to see him, then faced Gaston.

'You did well,' he said.

'I didn't,' Gaston murmured. 'That was the most expensive ten minutes of my life. The people in the house saw us even if the raiders didn't.'

'You're wrong. It was the most profitable ten minutes of your life. You've earned my gratitude, and that's worth ten times more than the gold in that bell.' Lincoln leaned forward. 'Now if you can use that devious mind of yours to work out how we can see off the rest of them, I might not arrest you.'

'I can't think,' Gaston murmured, rubbing his forehead in anger. 'It's taken me ten years to work out how I can get this gold, and now you've ruined everything in ten minutes.'

'Ten years since the last time the bell tolled, eh?' Lincoln mused. 'I reckon you've just earned yourself that reprieve.'

★　★　★

'We have to try again,' Richmond Cafferty said. 'We have enough cover out there.'

'That didn't help the dead men out there,' Lawrence Shannon said.

'Then the next ones will have to do better. We've already killed one of Francisco's guards. It's sure to get easier.'

Richmond looked around at the gathered raiders, and from his firm gaze Cameron reckoned he was expecting volunteers to step forward, but nobody did.

Lawrence noticed their lack of enthusiasm. 'We need to do this a different way.'

'How?'

Lawrence turned to look at his captives. He licked his lips, then moved off towards them. As Richmond followed him down the chapel, Cameron leaned towards Jack.

'This isn't looking good,' he said. 'We act now.'

Jack sighed then gave a brief nod.

'Look for an opening, then run for it.'

Cameron returned the nod, but said nothing else as Lawrence and Richmond stopped before the gathered captives.

'We need to get into the house, Raphael,' Lawrence said, his tone pleasant despite the coldness in his eyes.

'I can't help you,' Raphael said. He spread his hands. 'We will not raise our hands against our fellow man.'

'I know, but I'm sure there are *other* ways you can persuade Francisco to come out.'

Raphael narrowed his eyes. 'Other?'

The two men looked at each other until the force of Lawrence's glare made Raphael look away. Richmond caught the inference and paced round to stand before Lawrence.

'You'd better not be threatening to do what I think you are,' he said.

Lawrence set his feet wide apart. 'Ten years ago José Quintos wouldn't speak, no matter how much he suffered, but maybe this time his son will listen when it's others who are doing the suffering.'

'We agreed,' Richmond snapped, 'that when we got the gold we'd only take on anybody who stood in our way. These people aren't standing in our way.'

'When you provided Billy, Keating and me with such perfect alibis, did you really think this would end any other way?'

Richmond waved his arms as he struggled to find a response while behind Lawrence, Billy and Keating moved towards the captives, clearly being happy to carry out his orders.

'Wait!' Richmond snapped, raising a hand. 'I'll talk to Francisco. Maybe your threat will be enough to draw him out.'

'You have two minutes to talk him round. Then I start killing our hostages.' Lawrence's cold gaze roved over the assembled padres and other captives, and Cameron wasn't surprised when he picked out him and Jack. 'And

I'll start with those two.'

Richmond gave a curt nod that showed he was still unhappy with this plan. Then he turned briskly on his heels and hurried off down the chapel.

As Billy and Keating moved in to stand on either side of them, Cameron watched him go, willing him to be persuasive.

Richmond stopped beside the door to the courtyard.

'Don't shoot,' he shouted. 'I'm coming out to talk this through.'

Long seconds of their precious remaining time passed before a distant voice provided an answer. Then, with his hands raised to shoulder level, Richmond stepped out into the courtyard.

With him disappearing from view and his conversation being too far away to hear, Cameron stared at the doorway, unable to do anything but hope for good news.

When Lawrence announced the end of the first minute without Richmond returning from his negotiating, he forced himself to turn away.

Jack was staring into space, possibly preparing himself for a futile attempt to run to safety, and when he looked at the cruel-eyed Billy, he found no comfort there as the outlaw fingered the knife at his belt. So he looked over everyone's heads seeking to calm himself down.

Movement high up in the chapel caught his eye.

With the captives huddling in misery and the raiders forming a circle to guard them, he was the only one looking up to see it. At first he wasn't sure what he'd seen, thinking that maybe a bird had been trapped inside.

Then he realized what the movement had been.

A rope had been flung through a hole in the roof and had lassooed a broken end of an arch fifteen feet away. As he watched, the rope drew up tight to go taut against the side of the hole.

With a sigh he let his gaze drift back to Billy's glaring eyes, ensuring nobody noticed what he'd seen.

Marshal Lincoln Hawk hadn't been found and he must have hidden himself up there. Presumably he was planning something. He wished he could convey that to Jack and so give him hope, but he didn't dare risk trying to catch his eye.

Instead, he waited. Inexorably the deadline approached, every second counted down by Cameron's thudding heart, as beyond the circle of raiders Lawrence paced back and forth.

Beside him, Jack opened and closed his fists as he prepared to launch himself upon a doomed attempt to save them.

Then footfalls sounded and Lawrence jerked round to look at the chapel door and the returning Richmond.

'Is he coming out?' he asked.

'Not yet, but that was the first attempt,' Richmond said as he approached. 'We've established contact. Now we enter a waiting game and I reckon I — '

'If Francisco's waiting, we should give him something to listen to. Screams from the dying should test his resolve.'

'Don't,' Richmond said, raising a hand. 'This isn't the way it's supposed to happen.'

Billy, Lawrence and Keating swung round to face him.

'That's mighty interesting,' Lawrence said, sneering. 'Explain it to me.'

With the leaders having turned away Jack caught Cameron's eye then looked to the door, conveying that this was their only moment to act.

Cameron took a deep breath, torn between taking the chance and waiting to see how the disagreement amongst the leaders worked out. He nodded then rolled his shoulders, preparing himself to run, but then a booming sound echoed through the chapel.

The raiders silenced then drew their

guns as they sought out where the trouble was, but again the booming came.

This time Cameron realized what it was.

Up in the tower, Lincoln was tolling the bell.

14

'A bell,' Lawrence murmured while looking around. 'Why is someone striking a bell?'

His gaze alighted on Father Raphael who, with a shake of his body, got control of his own surprise.

'Nobody has tolled that bell in ten years,' he said. 'There's no way to get up there.'

Lawrence put a hand to an ear in a mocking fashion.

'And yet it rings.' Another long peel sounded, the tone dull and deep. 'How did someone get up there?'

'And who?' Billy asked.

'I have no idea.' Another boom sounded. 'But whoever it is, he appears to be striking it with enthusiasm.'

'That bell,' Lawrence said, 'used to summon help when there was trouble. It can be heard for miles around. We have to stop it.'

Nobody moved for two more rings until Raphael asked the question that had just occurred to Cameron.

'Have you people been here before?'

Lawrence snorted then paced up to Raphael.

'Who do you think tried to get the gold from José the last time?' he snarled as another loud peel sounded. 'I failed. Then I had to go away for a while, but now I'm back and this time there'll be no mistakes. I will leave with the gold.'

Lawrence glared at him as the bell continued to toll, its ominous off-key clanging making everyone look up to the roof and then towards the hole at the top of the area where the stairs had once been.

Cameron hoped nobody would wonder about the rope stretching to the arch, but as nobody else had looked to the roof before, they would probably think it had always been there.

With a determined stamp of a foot,

Richmond set out to take control of the situation.

He gestured for two men to go outside and see if they could see who was up there. In a clear demonstration that Richmond's status in the group had changed, these men looked at Lawrence for confirmation before they headed outside.

'So you led the bandit gang who tried to burn down the mission?' Raphael asked in a resigned manner.

'I did,' Lawrence said. 'So you'll know I mean to go through with my threats. And I intend to make sure your screams drown out that bell.'

'Then take me first.' Raphael dropped to his knees. 'When I meet my end with courage and humility it will give the others strength.'

Lawrence slapped a hand on Raphael's shoulder, moving to drag him to his feet, but he didn't get to complete whatever action he'd planned as Billy called out.

'Look!' he shouted, pointing.

'They're coming out!'

Everyone swung round to look down the chapel, and in the doorway beyond the statue the surviving guard trooped into view. He sported a bloodied bandage around his upper arm, but he kept his drawn gun on the men at the other end of the chapel.

Then Francisco walked in, his arrival making the raiders smirk. He and the guard looked around, surveying the scene. If they were seeking cover, the altar and statue was all that was available.

Then, to everyone's surprise, José followed them, but unlike the old and rambling man that Cameron had seen last night. Now he walked tall and unaided.

Francisco was looking at his father with concern, but also with admiration as the old man looked up towards the roof, an expression of benign satisfaction on his face. He listened to two tolls. Then he set off walking down the chapel towards them.

The guard moved to follow him, but Francisco raised a hand, commanding him to stay back.

The old man paced through the open space of the chapel towards the raiders, who moved apart to leave the leaders in the centre facing him.

'So you're not as ill as they say, old man,' Lawrence Shannon said.

José said nothing as he walked on, one steady pace at a time, every other pace appearing to fall in harmony with the steady ringing of the bell.

'You'd better be about to tell us where the gold is,' Billy said, 'or we'll do the worst thing you can imagine. We'll keep you alive. And what we did to you ten years ago will be like a warm bath compared to what you'll see us do to your son.'

José paced on, it now being clear that he was walking in rhythm with the ringing bell. He carried on until he was ten yards away from Lawrence.

Then with a stomp of his feet, as if he'd chosen this spot for a reason, he halted. He looked at each of the four men in the centre.

'You three I know,' he said, his voice calm and authoritative, 'but this one is new.'

'Richmond helped us,' Lawrence said, 'with a matter of law.'

'Helped?' Richmond murmured, shooting Lawrence an aggrieved glare, but Lawrence ignored him, having eyes only for José.

'And so it's time now for you, old man, to help us.'

'I couldn't help you ten years ago because you captured me before I got to my gun.' José smiled, then swung the end of his jacket aside to reveal the pearl-handled gun at his hip. 'But I have it now.'

Lawrence nodded, then shuffled his feet apart. Billy and Keating followed his action as did Richmond a few moments later.

The four men stood with confident gleams in their eyes and an arrogance in their stances that said they expected to triumph with ease in this showdown.

Throughout, the steady sounding of the bell sent its dull reverberations echoing through the chapel.

That previously unexpected sound had become familiar quickly and so everyone was attuned to its steady rhythm. So when the next peel was due and it didn't sound, the silence made everyone tense up and strain their hearing, waiting to hear the bell.

It didn't come and this made Lawrence glance up.

At that moment José threw his hand to his gun with a speed that belied his age and previous apparent infirmity. The leaders' confident expressions died a moment before the first one bit the dirt.

José hammered lead into Lawrence's chest, his unerring accuracy hitting him in the heart and sending him tumbling backwards before he'd even been able to draw. Then he swung his gun to the left, taking out Keating with a low shot to the guts as he dragged his gun from its holster.

Such was his speed he might have taken out all four men, but he darted his gun towards Richmond next. Only someone with lightning reflexes could have seen that Richmond hadn't gone for his gun but was instead raising his hands.

For a frozen moment they locked eye contact. Then José swung his gun the other way, aiming to shoot Billy, but he was too slow to complete the motion.

With only a split second to spare Billy drew his gun and tore off a quick shot that slammed low into José's ribs, making him spin round, stand for a moment, crouch, then keel over.

Then the shooting started.

Even with the demise of most of their leaders the raiders who were lining the walls peppered lead at the guard and Francisco at the other end of the chapel, making them scurry into hiding behind the statue.

With the only cover available being a few pews that had been pushed aside, some raiders ran for them while others crouched or lay down as they traded gunfire.

As the raiders weren't paying attention to their captives, Jack and Cameron took the opportunity to run for the fallen leaders.

They nudged past Richmond. Then each man moved to wrest a gun from dead fingers.

Slowly Richmond moved, his gaze drifting down to look at them.

'Stop right there,' he said.

*　★　★*

'You know what to do?' Lincoln said.

Gaston nodded. 'Start shooting and don't stop until we've got 'em all.'

'That sums it up.' Lincoln patted his back then grabbed the rope.

'And good luck.'

'Is that with seeing off the raiders or with getting myself killed so you can run off with the gold?'

Lincoln was pleased to see Gaston

flashed him an aggrieved look, suggesting he would at least complete his side of the plan.

Then he shuffled round to sit on the edge of the hole. Down below him was the centre of the chapel.

Nearly everyone had scurried into hiding behind pews, leaving only the bodies along with Cameron and Jack who were crouched down before Richmond. That sight was good enough for Lincoln to decide he'd go through with his reckless plan.

He shook the rope to ensure it would swing freely. Then, with a deep breath, he wrapped both hands around the rope, positioned himself directed towards Richmond's back, and kicked off into space.

He'd hoped that his push would let him swing down then slam into Richmond and so break his fall, but that thought fled his mind when he plummeted straight down.

He hurtled towards the chapel floor below, a giddy moment of panic overcoming him. Then to his relief the rope drew taut. It yanked his arms straight and let him swing down on the end of the rope, traversing in a long arc.

The air rushed by and he heard cries of surprise go up amidst the gunfire, presumably as people noted his progress. Ahead of him stood Richmond and at his feet Cameron and Jack were flinching as they looked up at him.

He also saw that he'd misjudged the length of the rope. His earlier crude measurement, along with the fact that Gaston had used the rope to climb the tower, had led him to believe it would be the right length. But at the bottom of his trajectory the rope would leave him dangling ten feet in the air.

Worse, he would pass five feet to Richmond's side.

He kicked out, hoping to redirect his path, but that only jerked him even further away from his target.

In an instant, he had to decide whether to let go or to carry on

swinging. Then he found that uncon-
sciously his body had taken that
decision away from him as he continued to clutch the rope in a death-like
grip. He went swinging on past
Richmond and then rose up into the
air.

Silence reigned in the chapel, the lack
of gunfire alerting him to the fact that
everyone had now seen him. He looked
down as he slowed to a halt thirty feet
up in the air and saw numerous faces
turned up towards him, staring in
bemused shock at the bizarre sight he
must be making.

Then the first person broke out of his
surprise and raised his gun to sight the
apparition that was now speeding
downwards again.

Lincoln heard gunfire but thankfully
it was wild. Then he was cheered to
see that he was swinging towards
Richmond, who was looking up at him,
his expression wide-eyed with shock on
seeing a man he thought dead swooping
down on him.

Richmond shook his shock away then moved for his gun, but he was already too late.

Lincoln released his grip and went plummeting down towards him. His feet hit him squarely in the chest, breaking his fall and then both men went tumbling.

When he came to rest, Lincoln was lying on his side, his bruised body jarred but otherwise intact. Richmond was lying pole-axed with his limbs splayed out, and beyond them the raiders had regained their wits and were turning their guns on him.

The nearest pew was ten feet away and so Lincoln gestured at Cameron and Jack to get into hiding. Then he pried Richmond's gun away and grabbed his shoulders.

He drew Richmond up to his chest as cover. This stilled the raiders' fire and so then walking backwards he dragged him into hiding beside Cameron.

'That entrance sure was something,' Cameron said.

'It worked well,' Lincoln said, 'but it'll only be worthwhile if we can get the rest.'

Cameron and Jack both nodded.

'We're with you,' Jack said.

Lincoln raised his gun.

'Then let's end this raid,' he said.

15

Lincoln beckoned for Cameron and Jack to spread out behind the pew then risked glancing over the top.

He judged that fifteen raiders were left, along with the surviving leader, Billy Maxwell. Standing against them were the three men behind the pew along with Francisco, his guard and Gaston.

With the raiders being in one place and the forces aligned against them being spread out at either end of the chapel and above, he reckoned they stood a good chance of prevailing.

He was about to begin firing when, at his feet, Richmond stirred.

'Is that really you, Lincoln?' he murmured.

'Sure,' Lincoln said, smiling. 'I bet you wish you'd stayed a bounty hunter now.'

'I've got plenty of regrets.' Richmond rubbed his chest ruefully.

'Like trusting Steven and Joshua to finish a job you should have completed?'

'That's not my biggest regret,' Richmond said in an honest sounding tone, 'and I reckon your tolling of the bell means you know what it is.'

Lincoln nodded. 'You didn't know Lawrence Shannon was the bandit who raided the mission ten years ago, did you?'

'Nope.' Richmond levered himself up to sit with his back to the pew. 'When I caught Lawrence he babbled a story about the gold to save his hide. I'd heard a hundred such tales, but this time . . . Twenty years of catching outlaws had got me money, but maybe one raid could get me ten times as much. So I used him. I got his gang back together, gave them alibis, but he was using me.'

'You were a fool not to realize that.'

'I was. I was tempted. I shouldn't have been, but I was. That was my first mistake.' He considered his gun in Lincoln's hand. 'But it doesn't have to be my last. Give me back my gun and I'll get Billy.'

Lincoln glanced down at Richmond's gun. He hefted it on his palm, fully intending to pocket it, but then a burst of gunfire tore along the top of the pew, spraying splinters.

Cameron and Jack risked bobbing up to return fire but they were forced to dive back down when another volley tore out.

'You've let me down plenty,' Lincoln said. 'First I thought you incompetent, then corrupt, now I know you're both.' Gunfire roared again, spraying splinters down on his head and this time making him flinch. 'But we're in a bad situation here, so get it right this time.'

He held out Richmond's gun. Richmond breathed a sigh of relief as he shuffled over and wrapped a hand around the gun. Then he swung round to adopt the same crouched position as the others had.

'Have you got a plan?' he asked.

'Keep 'em pinned down and hope we get lucky.'

Richmond shook his head. 'I'm finished no matter what happens next, so I reckon I'll use the more direct approach.'

He looked at Lincoln, appearing as if he wanted to say something more, perhaps even provide an apology. Then he turned away, rolled his shoulders, and sprang to his feet.

With a great roar he vaulted the pew and charged towards Billy.

His action was so suicidal and unexpected that he halved the distance before the raiders realized what he was doing. Then two men swung their guns up to shoot him, but Richmond had already thrust his gun out.

Twin shots roared, sending them reeling out of sight.

Three more men leapt up to take him on, but Richmond dispatched one with a high shot to the neck while Lincoln blasted the second through the chest.

Cameron and Jack joined him in shooting but their shots were wild, giving the final raider enough time to wing a slug into Richmond's side.

As Richmond folded over while still running on, Lincoln made the raider pay with two quick shots to the chest. Then he waited for the next man to show himself, but none did as Richmond's momentum let him stagger on and reach the pew.

Richmond slapped a hand on the top and half-fell, half-jumped over the pew to tumble out of sight.

Gunfire roared and Lincoln was pleased to see a raider jerk upwards into view as Richmond's shot found its target. Then another volley sounded, followed by silence and Lincoln didn't need to see what had happened to know that Richmond had done as much damage as he ever would.

'That was more than brave,' Jack said.

'I never expected that of him,' Cameron said.

Lincoln kept his thoughts to himself as he concentrated on the task in hand. Richmond's foolhardy run at the raiders had reduced their firepower, but it had yet to even up the battle.

For the next five minutes the groups exchanged sporadic gunfire with neither side making leeway but, trapped at the side of the chapel, the raiders became reckless.

One man ran towards the door until sustained gunfire beat him back and another man ran for a pew nearer to the altar and got a wounded arm for his trouble.

Lincoln decided to encourage their reckless behaviour with some taunting.

'Hey, Billy,' he called out, 'you ready to surrender?'

'We're leaving here with the gold, Lincoln,' Billy said. 'You did us a favour by letting us have more each.'

'The men left with you aren't thinking that. They're wondering if it's worth the risk when nobody has seen any gold and the only person who knew if there ever was any has been killed.'

Lincoln didn't know that for sure, but in a desperate situation some men will seize upon any chance to back down if it means they'll live.

'We know it's here. We're not giving up.'

'The offer is there. I'm only interested in you. Everyone else can walk away. All they have to do is say they're coming out and I won't fire.'

'We're not interested.'

'The offer wasn't for you. We won't shoot for a minute. Then you all get to die.'

Lincoln glanced at Cameron and Jack and winked. They returned a smile that said they understood Lincoln was attempting to sow discord.

Then they settled down to wait.

The minute passed slowly. Then the second minute dragged by as Lincoln gave the raiders even more time to worry themselves into fighting amongst themselves.

In recognition that he was still

around to help, Gaston tolled the bell with a firm blow.

Until now, Gaston hadn't taken advantage of his position to fire down at the raiders, and the sudden confirmation that Lincoln hadn't been the only man up in the tower had the desired effect.

'We're coming out,' a voice cried out, followed by two men standing from behind the pew. They cast an apologetic look at the men still hidden then, with their hands raised, they paced out into clear space.

Lincoln kept his promise and didn't fire, encouraging another man to stand. When the bell sounded again, this encouraged two more men to follow.

With them not being challenged, the men nearest the door accepted they were going to be allowed to get away and so they speeded up.

This persuaded the others behind them to break into a run. When several more men stood up with their arms raised, the developing rout proved too much for Billy. He jerked into view and, with a grunted oath, he slammed lead into the nearest man's back.

That man staggered sideways for several paces, blocking Lincoln's view of Billy, and that gave Billy enough time to swing round and shoot at the other surrendering men.

Most of them were fleeing through the door, but Lincoln didn't want to risk that these men might rejoin the fight and so he leapt to his feet.

'Cover me,' he ordered, then set off, not waiting to see if Cameron and Jack had heard.

He'd managed four paces following in Richmond's path when they started firing. Then Billy came into view.

Over twenty yards of the chapel floor the two men looked at each other. Billy jerked his gun arm to the side, but before he could fire Lincoln caught him with a running shot to the shoulder that sent him spinning away and out of view.

Another man jerked up from behind the pew to be faced with the sight of

Lincoln running towards him. The man swung his gun towards Lincoln, but as he fired, Lincoln caught him in the guts, knocking him backwards and into the wall. The man's gunshot wasted itself in the air.

With only one shot left before he'd have to reload, Lincoln reached the pew.

Only three men were on the other side and they raised themselves to take him on, but that only put them into Cameron's and Jack's view. Lead peppered at them. Unfortunately, Lincoln's helpers both aimed at the same man and this man spun away, repeatedly holed.

Luckily, Gaston chose that moment to make a timely break from striking the bell and he shot down at the second man. His gunshot slammed straight through the man's hat, leaving Lincoln to take on the final man.

As Lincoln vaulted the pew the raider fired up at him. Lincoln's quick motion ensured the shot flew wild, but when Lincoln returned fire while in mid air, his last shot was wild and cannoned into the wall.

He landed on the other side to see that everyone but this man and Billy were either dead or had surrendered. Then, without the time to reload his gun, he had no choice but to leap at the man.

He bundled into him before his assailant had a chance to fire and pushed him backwards into the wall, but the man wrapped an arm around him and kept him held close. The man's gun became trapped between their chests ensuring he didn't fire for fear of holing himself.

They strained back and forth with the man trying to tear himself away while Lincoln tried to keep them together. From down on the floor a hollow chuckle sounded.

Lincoln turned his attention from his tussle to look down and see that the bloodied Billy was smirking.

'You may have kept the gold from me,' Billy grunted through clenched teeth, 'but at least I get to see you die.'

From the corner of his eye Lincoln saw Billy roll on to his back. Then with a teeth-clenching effort Billy levered his arm up to aim his gun at him, but he didn't fire as he awaited a clear shot.

Lincoln struggled, aiming to force his assailant round to stand between them, but Billy's intervention had heartened the outlaw into reckoning he was getting the upper hand. He went limp and let Lincoln move him, but when he'd been swung round, he braced his back leg and continued the pivoting motion, spinning Lincoln away from him.

Lincoln teetered into clear space, and with that freeing the man's gun hand, he jerked his gun towards Lincoln. Repeated gunfire tore out, but to Lincoln's relief the man staggered forward, his back holed by Cameron's and Jack's gunfire.

The man pitched over, revealing Billy lying on his back, his gun aimed at Lincoln's chest. With only a moment to react, Lincoln hurled his gun at him.

The weapon struck Billy a glancing blow to the forehead. Then Lincoln leapt past the falling man.

All the air blasted from Billy's chest as Lincoln's bulky weight landed on him. With Billy winded, Lincoln grabbed his gun hand.

He held him down securely then strained to move the gun down to the floor. But his many exertions after his beating had weakened Lincoln too, and after pushing the gun down a foot he could move it no further.

Then slowly Billy got the upper hand as he forced his arm upwards.

Lincoln edged himself away from the advancing gun but that only had the effect of giving Billy more leverage. Billy speeded his movement, rolling himself on to his side as he swung the gun inexorably towards Lincoln's chest.

Lincoln put all his strength into trying to halt the advancing weapon, but still it moved closer, and he had to accept he couldn't stop its progress.

So he didn't try to.

He gritted his teeth and put on a good show of straining, making Billy grin, but just when Billy redoubled his efforts to make his growing advantage pay, Lincoln relaxed his grip and jerked backwards. Without the pressure keeping it back the gun swung wildly past Lincoln's chest and with Billy's arm being bent the gun slapped into his own belly.

A gunshot rang out, Billy clearly having decided to fire when he moved the gun. He and Lincoln locked gazes.

Billy opened his mouth to say something, but then his eyes glazed and he flopped down to lie still. Lincoln stared down at him until he was sure he was dead then stood up.

Cameron and Jack were making their way over to him as was Francisco. The raiders who had surrendered had all fled the chapel, and so with no one else to defeat, Lincoln walked away from

Billy and knelt beside Richmond's body.

He turned him over to find his still body had been holed repeatedly.

'You did well,' he said, 'in the end.'

16

'You need to be with him, Francisco,' Father Raphael said, stepping back from José's body.

'I thought he was dead,' Lincoln said, looking up.

Raphael shook his head.

'He's still with us,' he said, 'but not for long.'

As Raphael murmured and genuflected, Francisco sat beside his father.

'You didn't have to face them,' Francisco said.

'I did,' José said as he looked up at the roof. 'It's better to live for five minutes as a man than for a lifetime as what I was.'

'I know, but — ' Francisco lowered his head.

With a supreme effort José reached out and laid a hand on his arm.

'Don't grieve.' He rolled his head to

215

the side to raise an ear and smiled. 'It's good to hear the bell again. That's all I ever needed to bring me back. Make sure it never stops again.'

A flash of concern marred Francisco's eyes until he blinked it away. Gaston hadn't sounded the bell for a while, but clearly at the last José was hearing it.

Presently his breathing slowed then stopped. Francisco crouched over him, said a few words, then stood back to let Raphael complete his work.

With a visible wrench, he turned away to face Lincoln.

'I owe you a lot,' he said.

'Your father did the most.' Lincoln looked around, seeing that Cameron and Jack were joining the padres in checking on the bodies. 'So it'd honour his memory if you used that gold to carry out his dying wish and return the mission to its former state.'

'I'll do that.' Francisco looked up at the hole. 'It'll take a while to rebuild the steps, but I'll make sure the bell rings again.'

Lincoln followed his gaze. Then he looked down and smiled.

The rope he'd swung down on had come loose and was lying on the floor. He went over and picked it up.

'You already have someone up there who can ring the bell whenever you want, and this rope means he won't be going nowhere for a while.'

Francisco caught his meaning and provided a tense smile.

'That's why the gold was always safe up there. There's no easy way up or down unless you've got nerves of iron.'

Lincoln matched Francisco's smile. 'I reckon Gaston Prix will be testing those nerves before long.'

★   ★   ★

'You feeling sorry enough for what you did to us yet?' Cameron called up to the bell tower.

'It sure is a long way down,' Jack shouted when Cameron didn't get an answer. He waved the coiled length of

217

rope. 'And right now this rope will cost you seven hundred and fifty dollars.'

This taunt made Gaston lean out of the tower window.

'Go away,' he shouted with a dismissive wave while glaring down at them.

Cameron laughed. 'We're not going nowhere. We've got seven hundred and fifty dollars' worth of entertainment to get out of watching you get hungry and desperate.'

Gaston sneered at them before dropping down out of view. Then a dull peel of the bell sounded suggesting he'd slapped it in irritation.

This made both men laugh.

'I'm pleased to see you're happy,' Lincoln said, coming over to join them in looking up at the tower.

'We are,' Cameron said. 'But there's been enough cruelty here. We'll get the rope up to him . . . eventually.'

Lincoln nodded approvingly. 'That mean you're staying here?'

'All we ever wanted was to find work

and, with Francisco deciding to repair the mission, there'll be plenty available here. So we're staying.'

'Honest work is healthier than gambling against men like Billy Maxwell.'

'We sure learnt that. And you?'

'The raiders that fled didn't really expect me to let them get away. I won't disappoint them.'

'But at least you got the four leaders.'

Lincoln narrowed his eyes. 'There were *three* leaders. Never forget that. Three outlaws and a bounty hunter.'

'But before Richmond went and — '

'Richmond was a legendary bounty hunter and you were privileged to have seen him in action. That's the way you'll tell it if anyone asks.' He leaned forward. 'I mean, how do you know he wasn't working undercover and everything you thought you saw and heard was for show?'

Cameron and Jack glanced at each other in a sceptical fashion. Then Cameron faced Lincoln and shrugged.

'I guess,' he said, 'all that matters is

that in the end he did the right thing.'

That comment made Lincoln smile. Then he tipped his hat to them and turned away to head to his horse.

Both men watched the lawman trot away then speed up to a gallop as he headed off to track down the surviving raiders of the Mission San Juan.

Above them, Gaston tolled the bell.

THE END

We do hope that you have enjoyed reading this large print book.

Did you know that all of our titles are available for purchase?

We publish a wide range of high quality large print books including:
Romances, Mysteries, Classics
General Fiction
Non Fiction and Westerns

Special interest titles available in large print are:
The Little Oxford Dictionary
Music Book, Song Book
Hymn Book, Service Book

Also available from us courtesy of Oxford University Press:
Young Readers' Dictionary
(large print edition)
Young Readers' Thesaurus
(large print edition)

For further information or a free brochure, please contact us at:
Ulverscroft Large Print Books Ltd.,
The Green, Bradgate Road, Anstey,
Leicester, LE7 7FU, England.
Tel: (00 44) **0116 236 4325**
Fax: (00 44) **0116 234 0205**

A MAN NAMED SHONTO

Ryan Bodie

They were already hanging Marshal Holder when Shonto rode into town. It was one hell of a welcome for a loner with a gun but Shonto sensed that things were going to get even worse. He was right. The marshal's body was still swinging from the cottonwood across the street from his own jailhouse when the town became a bloody battleground. At that point, Shonto had just two choices: shoot to kill or join the lawman in hell.

THE DEVIL's GOLD

M. Duggan

Dennis Rumble wasn't a good man — but he wasn't entirely bad — unlike the notorious band of outlaws calling themselves the Coyotes, into whose territory he was obliged to travel. He was on a mission to rescue a beautiful woman snatched from the stage by the outlaws. But things are not always as they seem. Twists and turns lay ahead of him and many men were destined to lose their lives over what Rumble called 'The Devil's Gold'.

ROBBERY IN SAVAGE PASS

D. M. Harrison

Soames Ho accepts work from a Pinkerton agent, to take gold from Marysville to a Californian bank. But the driver of the stagecoach carrying the gold is nervous; the shotgun rider a greenhorn. They travel through Savage Pass, only to face three men intent on robbery. But the Pinkerton agent's deliberate plan, to have an ineffectual escort for the stagecoach, underestimates Soames. He believes in justice, and whatever the cost, he's determined to find the gold and the outlaws.

THE LEGACY

Logan Winters

There was nothing special about the J-Bar ranch in Colorado . . . except that it had thirty thousand acres of prime land and its previous owner had just been murdered, leaving $50,000 in hidden gold. Then the whole territory joined the hunt for the missing fortune; violence and murder became commonplace. But then three heirs arrived from the East — and that is when true chaos erupted . . .

WIND RIDER

Thomas McNulty

The Sioux call him Wind Rider . . .
Hank Benteen rides into trouble in a
Wyoming valley after saving the lives
of a homesteader and his children. A
range war is brewing and some of
the cowboys are hiding a murderous
secret. Then, resolving to safeguard
the homesteaders' properties, Benteen becomes involved in a deadly
game with two avaricious men, intent
on acquiring land by brute force.
The Wind Rider will need all his
skills as a gunman to survive . . .